Waking Up Wed

—

Christy Jeffries

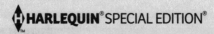

HARLEQUIN® SPECIAL EDITION®

Recycling programs
for this product may
not exist in your area

ISBN-13: 978-0-373-65941-8

Waking Up Wed

Copyright © 2016 by Christy Jeffries

HARLEQUIN®
www.Harlequin.com

Printed in U.S.A.

Christy Jeffries graduated from the University of California, Irvine, with a degree in criminology and received her Juris Doctor from California Western School of Law. But drafting court documents and working in law enforcement was merely an apprenticeship for her current career in the dynamic field of mommyhood and romance writing. She lives in Southern California with her patient husband, two energetic sons and one sassy grandmother. Follow her online at christyjeffries.com.

Books by Christy Jeffries

Sugar Falls, Idaho

A Marine for His Mom

To Betty Lou Astleford,
a consummate peacemaker who also ran off
and got married despite her mother's warnings that
if she married "that man," he would never be able
to afford shoes for her children.

Your strong marriage was a priceless gift to your
family and worth far more than all the shoes
you bought us to prove your mother wrong.
And you *really* taught me how to splurge on
a good pair of shoes. I love you, Momoo.

Chapter One

Every morning for the first thirty years of her life, Kylie Chatterson had woken up alone.

Until today.

She'd barely rolled over on the hotel's plush mattress when her sleepy eyes did a double take at the fair-haired, angelic-looking man snuggled up beside her.

Who in the world was he—and how in the world had he gotten here?

His muscular body was chiseled like the marble statue of a Greek god, but this work of art was warmer and much more real. The brutal morning sun intruded through the wide-open curtains she'd obviously neglected to close, shedding unnecessary light on her growing sense of shame.

Kylie held her breath, commanding her body to stay still so her spinning head could add up all the facts.

Fact one. She'd flown to Reno for her friend's coed

bachelor/ette party yesterday. This was definitely the room she'd checked into because her fuchsia cheetah-print suitcase was haphazardly propped on the luggage rack at the foot of the bed. So at least she was where she was supposed to be. That was good.

Fact two. She remembered meeting up with some of the wedding party and having one or two cocktails in the casino bar. She normally didn't drink much, so it couldn't have been more than a couple. Could it? She spotted three plastic oversize souvenir cups by the TV stand. That wasn't so good, but it explained the throbbing at the base of her scalp, her queasy stomach and her lack of memory.

Don't feel, she commanded herself. *Just think and solve the problem.*

Fact three. There was a dyed-blue carnation bouquet next to an instant photo in a cheesy cardboard frame from the Silver Rush Wedding Chapel that read Hitched in Reno on the bedside table next to her. The image was too grainy—or maybe her eyes were too fuzzy to see—but she was definitely the one holding up the ugly flowers in the picture. She carefully stretched out her arm, trying to bring the photograph closer and into focus without waking the sleeping Adonis beside her. She squinted at the photo. Had they gone to some sort of Wild West–themed bar last night? Maybe that was where she'd met the guy next to her, because he was in the picture, too.

She let out a quiet breath while she carefully studied the shot for more clues. She and Mr. Adonis looked as if they were sitting in a covered pioneer wagon. Next to them sat two people wearing costumes reflecting Nevada's silver mining heritage. At least she hoped those were costumes. This was really weird, unless...

She glanced over her bare shoulder. The perfectly formed male snored softly away in her bed, and, as she let her gaze drift past the golden features of his face, she rethought her earlier angel appraisal. There was nothing cherubic about the man from the neck down. Had some of the bachelorettes ended up at an all-male revue show?

Oh, no. What if this guy next to her was a male stripper and she'd hooked up with him? Her parents would be mortified. They'd raised her to be a strong woman with an even stronger sense of self-worth—one who would never get taken advantage of by a man.

She dropped the photo and wiped her damp palm on the sheet. Kylie was a certified public accountant and she needed an explanation for this situation that would add up, one that would make sense. She had to stop jumping to conclusions and get back to her usual analytical approach to problem solving.

Besides, his body might look as though it could grace the cover of one of her historical romance novels, but his relaxed face looked too innocent to work for tips.

She rubbed her eyes before scrutinizing the picture again. Regardless of where they were or who else was in the photo with them, they'd both looked pretty darned pleased with themselves last night. Obviously, they'd had a fun time. She didn't know if that was good or not.

Fact four. She was still dressed in her matching blue lace panty and bra set—but nothing else. What did that mean? Had they or hadn't they…?

Again, she looked at her bedmate. She had no idea what he had on underneath the covers, but on top, he was wearing nothing but an impressive array of bronzed muscles and a smile. The heat of embarrassment shot up her cheeks.

Even though most people thought Kylie dressed too flashy and went out on more than her fair share of dates, the reality was that in all of her thirty years, she'd never let a man get past second base. And now she couldn't remember who the batter was or whether he'd hit a home run last night! She didn't need to be sober to come to the conclusion that winding up half naked and in bed with a stranger couldn't be good at all.

Before she could move on to fact five, the blond Adonis snuggled closer and wrapped his overdeveloped biceps around her waist. His warm strength sizzled against her taut skin, and it took every fiber of her normally calm demeanor to not leap off the bed and run away from him. She no longer had time to be analytical. If she tried to appraise the situation any more, she'd end up waking him. Maybe she could just sneak out quietly.

Wait. This was *her* room.

She might bite her tongue when some of the more gossipy women in town mocked her, but having grown up the only girl with four older brothers and an opinionated father, she was used to establishing her independence and her individuality. She was no wallflower. Kylie had learned early on that in life she needed to stand up for herself in order to stand out. She'd also learned how hold her own with men. Even gorgeous, naked ones.

She shoved at his shoulder. "Pssst."

His only response was to grip her tighter.

"Hey," she said louder as she tried gracefully to extricate herself from his embrace.

His full pink lips nuzzled against her neck, and a shocking tingle raced down her spine.

The intimate contact both aroused and startled her. She used her bare leg to shove herself away from him. Unfortunately, her heel nailed him in the shin and, just as she was pushing away, he yelped and scrambled backward. The force of his retreat timed perfectly with her launch, and she lost her momentum, collapsing to the patterned carpeted floor in a pile of long limbs and blue lace.

"What in the hell?" she cried out, trying to pull the sheet down to cover herself.

"Where am I?" he asked.

With the sheet finally wrapped around her, Kylie got to her feet so she could confront the equally confused stranger sitting up in her bed. She caught sight of her makeshift toga in the dresser mirror and lifted her chin higher. Her friends always told her that with her tall, curvaceous body, she looked just like an auburn version of Wonder Woman. Yet right now the resemblance was more similar to the superhero's secret identity, Princess Diana, who needed to defend her Amazon kingdom from unwanted males. "I'll tell you *where* you are if you tell me *who* you are."

"I'm Andrew." He rubbed at his close-cropped haircut, and she took comfort in the fact that his head must be pounding just as badly as her own.

Andrew didn't sound like a stripper name—not that she had any point of reference when it came to exotic male dancers.

"Well, Andrew, you're in my room at the Legacy Casino in Reno. Don't ask me how you got here, because I'm still pretty fuzzy on the details."

The man looked at the disheveled bedding, then back at her, his eyes traveling the length of her body before settling on her heated face. He blinked a couple of times before his hand fumbled on the nightstand and lifted a pair of wire-framed lenses to his eyes.

"You're Kylie," he said, recognition apparently dawning on him.

"Well, at least one of us knows…" She faltered as a flashback from last night triggered her own memory bank. "You know, with those glasses on, you kind of look like that military friend of Cooper's…"

His nod confirmed the sudden fear she couldn't even bear to say aloud. Oh, no. This was bad. This was very, very bad.

"Oh, my gosh." She pointed an accusatory finger at him while he looked around the room sheepishly, probably in search of his holy vestments. Or at least his pants. "You're the minister who's performing the wedding. You're Drew Gregson!"

Snippets of yesterday afternoon clicked into place, and she remembered arriving at the cocktail lounge early so she could welcome the rest of the wedding party. Drew, the groom's best friend, was already there and looking as lost and as confused as a lamb. And she'd apparently led him straight to slaughter. She sank down into the nearest chair. He hadn't stood up yet, and she wasn't about to get in bed again with a man of the cloth. "We are so going to hell."

Yesterday she'd ordered him a drink, telling him it would help him relax. Then she'd cracked a ribald joke to loosen the tension. He'd made a scandalized face before laughing, and they'd toasted the newlyweds. Everything after that was a blur. A horrible, sinful blur.

"Yes, that's me. But I'm not a minister."

She studied his face, trying to decide if he was telling the truth or just doing damage control. Maybe he was used to waking up in strange hotel rooms with women he didn't know, but he didn't seem too concerned about the fate of their eternal souls. So if he wasn't a pastor, then what was he? And why was he so unbelievably calm—and not the least bit modest?

She averted her eyes because if she had to look at his rock-hard abs any longer, she would have no hope of keeping her mind focused and figuring out how everything had gone so completely wrong last night. "Can you please put a shirt on or something?"

He pulled the comforter off the floor and dragged it around his body as he scanned the room. Any article of male clothing would do at this point, but Kylie had no idea where he'd left his. From her vantage point, she tried to look around the room, too, but her search kept returning to his bare torso and the fabric secured around his waist with his left hand. After years of being single, she resorted to her default training and zoned in on the shiny gold ring.

"What the hell is that?" She pointed to the offending object. "You're married! I just spent the night with a drunk, married man."

She pulled her white four-hundred-thread-count shroud tighter around her body, as if she could make herself vanish from the shame and his anonymous wife's impending wrath.

"What are you talking about?" Drew asked as he picked up a plain white undershirt and pulled it on over his head. "I'm not married."

"You're wearing a wedding ring."

He squinted his baby-blue eyes at his finger, looking truly puzzled by the gleaming jewelry. Then he turned his bespectacled gaze to her as if waiting for her to explain the whole situation to him.

Well, she certainly had no idea what was going on. Still, his appraising look was patient and intense, and Kylie had the feeling that Drew had probably won his fair share of staring contests. His continuing focus unnerved her, and her trembling fingers slipped on the sheet. She struggled to get her improvised garment back into position, and her breath hitched when she saw what had caught his attention.

"You have one, too." His tone was casual, lacking any judgment or accusation.

She stared at the matching band on her own ring finger. For the first time in history, Kylie Chatterson, former pep leader of the Boise State Cheer Team, second runner-up for Miss Idaho USA and current CPA whiz, was at a loss for words.

Her sheet slipped to the floor unnoticed as she ran into the bathroom and slammed the door.

Maybe she wasn't being very mature and rational about this situation—whatever *this* situation was—but she felt as though she couldn't breathe, and her palms were sticky with sweat.

This must be what a panic attack felt like. Or a hangover. Ugh, how much *had* she had to drink last night?

Don't freak out. Where was her inner voice of reason when she needed it most? Probably back in the hotel lounge where she must've accidentally dumped it out of her designer gold clutch, along with the rest of her morals, when she'd pulled out her credit card to pay for that first round.

She took a sip of water from the sink, then held one hand under the cool flow while she forced herself to inhale and exhale through her nose and slow her breathing. When it finally felt as if her lungs weren't going to explode, she shut off the faucet and dried her hands.

She needed to think. Why was she wearing this stupid wedding ring, and why had Drew Gregson spent the night in her room? The answer was obvious to her methodical and organized brain, even if she was completely unclear on how they'd gotten to this point.

She stared at her sloppy reflection in the mirror, as if the hot mess looking back at her could provide any explanation. Her long auburn curls were a tangled disaster and her once carefully applied makeup had probably been left behind on one of the ten pillows out there with the Angel of Lust.

Thankfully, she'd unpacked yesterday afternoon and

had left her toiletry kit on the bathroom counter. She pulled the fluffy white hotel robe off the hook and double-knotted it around her waist. After running a brush through her hair and securing it into a tight ponytail, she scrubbed her face clean. She brushed her teeth much longer than the American Dental Association recommended, knowing she was stalling for time.

Just as she rinsed out the last of the toothpaste, a knock sounded at the bathroom door. "Uh, Kylie?"

Great. He was still out there. She needed to get rid of him ASAP so she could get down to the business of figuring out just what in the world was going on around here.

"I just found some papers on the dresser," he said through the locked barrier between them. "I think we may have a little situation."

Drew's head felt as if mortar rounds were ricocheting inside his skull. The marriage license trembling in his normally steady hands looked real enough, but his hazy eyes could barely make out the words. He looked at his watch. Oh nine hundred. He needed to pick up his nephews in less than twenty-four hours. His twin brother's eight-year-olds were waiting for him at his parents' house in Boise.

At least he was now dressed and could face the unexpected crisis that had barricaded herself in the bathroom with a little decorum—unlike the behavior he must've exhibited last night. He'd found the last of his clothes strewn about as if a bomb had detonated in the hotel room. He was usually so neat and took care with his clothing. Of course, he also took care not to overindulge in alcohol or marry women after knowing them for all of five hours.

Clearly, he wasn't himself.

For the past ten minutes, he'd been trying to remain cool and controlled while simultaneously racking his foggy brain for details on how he'd ended up in bed with the beautiful woman. Thankfully, she'd run into the bathroom. He hoped she would get dressed because, even for a man who'd sworn off women, there was only so much temptation he could handle.

Yesterday afternoon, the building anxiety and uncertainty about becoming his nephews' legal guardian while his brother deployed on a top secret mission this summer had swelled to an all-time high. It didn't help that Drew was suffering from jet lag, having arrived fresh off the cargo plane from a military base in the Middle East. To top it all off, he was about to embark on a new assignment as the staff psychologist at the naval hospital near his hometown. It was a trifecta of pressure he hadn't been expecting.

He shook his head. Regardless, all the compounding mental and physical effects weren't an excuse for what he'd done—if only he knew what exactly that was. He'd counseled numerous soldiers and sailors about the healthy and effective ways of handling stress stateside after returning from war. He was pretty sure that getting drunk and marrying the first woman he met wasn't one of his usual recommendations.

Drew remembered introducing himself to Kylie at the cocktail lounge in the casino yesterday before the rest of the wedding party arrived. He'd been eager to see his buddy Matt Cooper, who was marrying Kylie's best friend, Maxine Walker. In fact, Drew had indirectly introduced the bride and groom when he'd coerced Cooper to participate in a military pen pal program with Maxine's son.

Yesterday, emotions had been running high for everyone. For Drew they'd been coupled with the unknown anxiety of what awaited him at home.

Kylie had been so friendly and so easy to talk to. As a

psychologist, Drew was accustomed to listening to other people's problems and giving guidance or counsel whenever necessary. But he'd never been the one on the couch, so to speak, and wasn't used to venting his own feelings. She'd made a joke about him needing a drink to loosen up, and he'd thought, *What could one glass hurt?*

He eyed the neon-green oversize souvenir cups shaped like slot machines and then ran a hand over his aching head. What could it hurt, indeed? Those deceiving fruity concoctions packed a punch he wouldn't soon forget.

He stared at the Hitched in Reno photo tossed on the nightstand and wondered how many souvenir cups it had taken for him to get so loopy that he'd thought saying wedding vows before God and a couple of character actors dressed in silver miners' garb was a good plan.

But he looked beyond the Boomtown theme of the photo of him in his starched jeans and Kylie in her miniskirt, noting the matching smiles on their faces. They may have been three sheets to the wind, but they looked genuinely happy. Almost blissful.

He'd attended his share of weddings and, while many were joyful events, some had been clad in scandal or anger or forced circumstances. In this picture, though, he and Kylie were looking at each other with such unadulterated elation, he went through his catalog of memories to recall if he'd ever seen a couple look as happy on their wedding day as he and Kylie had.

He'd always had an idea of marriage in the back of his mind and knew he'd tie the knot someday. His father was a minister and often preached about honoring the vows of marriage. Maybe because he was old-fashioned or maybe because of his religious upbringing, Drew knew that when he finally settled down, it would be only once. In fact, right after graduate school, he'd thought Jessica could have potentially be the one. He'd wanted to take his time, draw out their courtship, because he needed to be positive that they were perfect for each other. Turned out Jessica hadn't liked waiting for his decision.

After that, he'd vowed not to enter into any relationship—even a sexual one—with a woman without ensuring she was marriage material. He'd thought taking a break from women would be a simple test of mind over matter.

But now his self-imposed rule was being seriously tested as it never had been before. He looked down at the wedding photo and the attractive redhead in the too-tight outfit and too-high heels. Not that Drew believed in stereotypes of any kind, but Kylie didn't look anything like the spouses of some of his esteemed colleagues. He remembered thinking she was stunning when he'd met her yesterday, even if her attire was not what one would describe as conventional. Then, this morning, when she'd dropped her sheet and he'd seen her in all her womanly glory, he'd had a difficult time looking away.

Despite his promise to himself, he struggled with the same carnal feelings that most people did. But up until now, he'd been able to control his emotions. Besides, living in battle-ready military installations around the world for the past few years had limited the potential for temptation, as his social interactions with single women who weren't wearing unisex camouflage had been few and far between.

Yet Kylie's style and personality were so animated and so colorful, he couldn't help but be drawn to her.

The water in the bathroom shut off again and he braced himself for her to exit. They would have to come to terms with what they'd done.

The door opened and she held her freshly scrubbed face high, but even the oversize bathrobe couldn't do much to diminish the endowments she'd been blessed with.

She leaned against the door frame, her green, makeup-free eyes squeezed tightly closed. "Please don't tell me what I think you're going to tell me."

"If you think I'm going to tell you that this wedding picture was just a joke, then I won't tell you that."

"How do you know?" She squinted one lid open, and he handed over the very official-looking marriage license. Sign, sealed and delivered.

She was a smart woman. Drew couldn't recall how he knew this, but he remembered thinking it at some point last night. So he remained quiet and let her come to the inevitable conclusion.

"Wow." She sank down to the floor, her long, shapely legs exposed as her knees poked through the gap in the white terry cloth.

He'd learned early on that to have effective communication with people, he needed to reach them on their level. So despite the queasiness in his own stomach, he gingerly lowered himself to floor beside her.

"I'm sorry," he said, wanting to comfort her. "I don't know how it happened or why we did it, but it looks as though we're married."

She cupped her head in her hand while holding the license in the other. Her eyes traveled over the paper repeatedly, probably looking for some loophole or some hint that it wasn't legitimate. Unfortunately, Drew knew they were staring at the real deal.

"But how can we be married when it says our only witnesses were two people who signed their names as Pistole Pepe and Maddog Molly?"

Drew handed over the wedding photo. "I think that guy with the long beard and miner's hat is Pistole. This snarling woman holding the blue flowers like yours must be Molly."

"God, my maid of honor was an overweight saloon girl with a missing tooth."

"Maybe we should try to focus on the more important facts," he suggested.

"Seriously? How can you not be worried about this?" The arched red brow made him think she didn't like his suggestion. "You got totally wasted last night and forced a complete stranger to marry you. Who the hell knows what kind of fornication we committed in that bed right over there? Yet now you have the nerve to tell me that none of that is important?"

"Okay, let's recap. One, I'm a doctor. A clinical psychologist, to be exact. My job is to look at the big picture."

"But you're performing the wedding. Don't you have to be a preacher to do that?"

"Uh, no. Anyone can get certified online to do that. I owed Cooper a favor and he knows I hate public speaking."

"Well, that explains that mystery." She let out a sigh, then leaned her head back so quickly, it thunked against the wall.

"Can we get back to the current situation?" He waited for her to nod before continuing, "Two, I don't think it's in anybody's best interests to keep a running tab of potential sins. Three, I might have been somewhat intoxicated, but judging by the smile on your face in that picture, I think we can safely say that nobody forced anybody to do anything last night. Four, I'm pretty sure that whatever might or might not have happened in that bed last night wouldn't be considered fornication if we were technically married."

Drew was a patient man, but he didn't know if the woman collapsed in front of him was willing to listen to reasonable logic. How would he? He didn't know her from Adam. Or Eve. But he *did* know that if Eve had looked anything like Kylie Chatterson, Drew didn't blame Adam one bit for taking a bite of that cursed apple.

"I'll concede points one through three," she finally said. "But since you're not a minister, then you're clearly no expert on what might or might not constitute fornication."

Wait, now she was annoyed that he *wasn't* a minister? The lady needed to make up her mind, because he couldn't win this game. "Are you an attorney?"

"No, I'm a CPA. When you talk in numbers to me, things make better sense."

Drew would have to store that knowledge away for future use. "Listen, I'm just as confused and overwhelmed by this whole thing as you are. But I know that we have to keep our heads clear and our words civil if we're going to get through this."

She nodded, but her confused eyes still sought answers. "How can you be so calm? This can't be great news for you, either, but you've yet to freak out."

"Job hazard. I'm in the business of keeping calm when everything around me is blowing up. Literally."

"Well, this would certainly qualify as an explosion in my life." The back of her head thumped against the wall again as she lifted her face to the ceiling.

"There's a coffeemaker in here. Why don't I brew some and we can figure out our next course of action?"

He stood and held out his hand to her. He realized his mistake when she stared at his extended fingers before taking several breaths. He was still wearing the gold band. She probably didn't appreciate the reminder of last night, but he hadn't been able to get the thing off his oversize knuckle.

At almost six foot four and weighing close to two hundred thirty pounds, Drew was a big man. He was accustomed to things not always being available in his size.

Apparently, his selection in wedding rings was no exception.

After a few uncomfortable moments, she finally accepted his extended hand by placing her own in his. He effortlessly pulled her up and, when they were practically face-to-face, he was pleasantly surprised that she was only a few inches shorter than him.

But holding hands made it easier for her to study the his-and-hers duplicate set of jewelry. She dropped his fingers as if the rings were some sort of live grenades and then tugged on her gold band, but it wouldn't even budge.

"Ugh. It's stuck. I'm probably swollen up from all the booze."

Drew's eyes dipped from her hand to her heaving chest as she labored over the ring, and he noticed her fingers weren't the only things swollen. The way the lapel of her robe gaped open, he could see that her breasts were about to spill out of their D cups.

Heat stole up his neck, and his skin tightened all over his body. He quickly turned away to walk toward the mini-brewer tucked into a corner alcove.

With his back to her, he heard her cross behind him to the opposite side of the room. He hoped she wasn't physically distancing herself in fear that he was some sort of pervert and might attack her. She probably sensed the way his body was responding to her, and he couldn't blame her for taking precautions.

"We're supposed to meet the rest of the wedding party for brunch in less than thirty minutes," she said as he made the first cup. "Do you think they'll wonder whether something is wrong if neither one of us shows?"

"Why wouldn't we show up for bunch? I, for one, am starving. Did we even have dinner last night?"

"Don't ask me," Kylie said, then thanked him for the

mug he offered. She sat in one of the chairs, and he wondered if her legs were as shaky as his. "After we left the cocktail lounge, everything else that happened last night is pretty vague. And what do you mean 'why *wouldn't* we show up for brunch'? We can't walk in there, in front of all our friends, and act as if nothing's out of the ordinary."

"Why can't we? They obviously weren't there last night or they would've put a stop to…you know." Drew gestured toward the empty souvenir cups littering the hotel room, leaving any mention of the impromptu wedding unsaid.

"That's a good point. So you think we should just act as if nothing happened? I mean, I don't want to lie to my friends, but if we play everything off as though we had a bit too much to drink and don't remember last night clearly, that would be the truth, right?"

Drew had been raised to believe that an omission was just as serious as a lie. But it wasn't as though he needed to broadcast their mistake to the world or make it anyone's business. He didn't know what to do. Nothing about this situation was sitting well. Including the way Kylie's sweet green eyes pleaded with him.

He was a problem solver by nature and wished he could just give her some advice and then walk away. But this was one problem he didn't know how to solve.

"Can I ask you a question?" He took off his glasses and rubbed the bridge of his nose.

"Sure, but I can't guarantee I'll know the answer."

"What are your thoughts on marriage? Not this marriage, per se, but in general. I mean, you're an attractive woman. You're smart. And clearly, you know how to have fun. So is there a reason why you're not married?"

She sank her head back against the chair as if the question exhausted her. But Drew was used to waiting for people to explain things in their own ways. So he stood there, gripping his coffee mug and glasses, waiting for her answer.

"I really have no idea why I'm not married. Heaven knows I've dated enough men that you'd think I would've found Mr. Right by now." That wasn't exactly the answer Drew was hoping to hear. Sure, Kylie was pretty, and he could see why any red-blooded male would want to go out with her, but he could've done without the knowledge that had an active dating calendar.

"To me, marriage is a serious commitment," he said, trying to make a point.

"Which we entered into lightly." Kylie's posture, even when seated, was tall and impressive, and Drew doubted she could sit up any straighter.

"But still, we entered into it and everything it entails."

"Listen, I get it that not everyone believes in divorce. But I'm sure we can get an annulment or something that wouldn't taint your beliefs or your reputation."

"Some people might see that as a solution. Yet I have a feeling that we took vows before God."

Kylie looked ready to bolt and probably would've run as far from him as she could if he wasn't standing in between her and her suitcase full of clothes. "We also took vows before some guy named Pistole Pepe, which I'm sure wasn't his legal name at birth. Look, you seem like a real straitlaced guy, but there's an exception to every rule."

Maybe. Kylie looked like the kind of woman who was used to making her own rules. Yet something about her fighting spirit made him question whether he wanted an exception. "I don't know much about the legal logistics, but can we get an annulment if we consummated the marriage?"

Her charming face blushed more crimson than he would've thought possible, and he wanted to kick himself for embarrassing the poor woman. She was definitely shyer than she let on.

Despite the heat staining her cheekbones, she sat up even straighter. But her voice was a mere whisper when she finally spoke. "Did we...?"

Once again, he wanted to put her fears to rest, but he honestly had no idea. He felt like a complete idiot for not remembering. But the fact remained that they'd gotten married and they'd woken up together nearly naked. And did he mention that since he'd sworn off intimacy with women, he hadn't had sex in over a year?

"Honestly," he said, "I don't know. And if neither one of us knows the answer to that, then I'm guessing we also don't know whether or not we used...um...protection?"

Chapter Two

"Oh, my gosh. No. No. No." Kylie thought of every curse word ever uttered by her father and four athletic brothers, and then repeated one that would have shocked a war-weary sailor, let alone the confused doctor in front of her.

"Sorry," she mumbled. She hated offending Drew, who finally looked uncomfortable. It wasn't his fault she'd sacrificed her much-practiced poise for the feistiness she usually kept hidden. "I don't usually talk like that. I didn't mean to let my mouth get away from me."

He looked at her lips and she instantly regretted the words that drew his attention there. But she was too absorbed in her own panic to worry about what kind of pleasure they might or might not have partaken of last night.

"I know we wouldn't have forgotten *that*. Right?" She was too mortified to even say what *that* was.

He ran his hand through his close-cropped military-style haircut, and she wondered how she could have possibly thought this conservative, clean-cut man in the crisp jeans and J.Crew sweater was a male stripper.

"I would like to think that we both would have known better than to be so reckless." His confident tone didn't quite match his puzzled and slightly pink expression. "Yet from the looks of everything else around us, we should have known better about a lot of things."

"But you don't understand. I can't just be married. Or suddenly pregnant by someone I don't know. My father would kill me. My brothers would kill *you*. Everyone in Sugar Falls would say they knew something like this was bound to happen. I'll have to give up my accounting practice and move to Boise. Wait. Farther than that. Siberia, maybe. This is going to ruin my whole life."

"Well, at least we're equally screwed."

Wait, had he just said *screwed*? Perhaps the gravity of the situation was finally sinking in for Doctor Perfect.

"I mean, it's not as if this is going to look really great for my career or my family." He waved his arm dramatically at the room, including the empty beverage cups and her. "I'm not exactly proud of all this."

It was difficult to not take the insult personally. Why would he be ashamed of marrying her? Maybe she wasn't some stuffy Miss Priss, but she was decent in the looks department and she was financially successful. Plus, she didn't have any standout mental health concerns, addictions or genetic diseases—that she knew of. Frankly, he could do a lot worse.

Of course, so could she. And hadn't she proved just that with some of the losers she'd dated in the past? No man she'd ever been out with—and if you asked her two best friends, they'd say she'd been out with a lot—had made it past her rigid checklist of qualities for Mr. Right. Her strike-one-and-you're-out policy explained why she went through eligible men so quickly. That and her fear of taking home anyone to meet her opinionated family.

While life had taught her to be pragmatic about most things, Kylie believed in true love. She was a romantic at heart and knew that somewhere out there, her soul mate was waiting for her. Unfortunately, she doubted that her soul mate would want the pregnant ex-wife of some military shrink.

She sighed. "I'm sorry if it seems as if I'm only looking out for my best interests here. This probably wasn't exactly what you envisioned, either, when we ordered that first round last night. But at least you don't live in a small, judgmental town like Sugar Falls. You won't be carrying around a nine-month reminder of this night or have smug busybodies shake their heads at you when you pass them on the street with your love child in tow. You get to hop on the first navy plane out of here and go on about your life."

Drew knelt in front of her, his fingers cupping her chin, gently forcing her to meet his eyes. "I'm not going anywhere. Especially if you're carrying my child. You don't know me or the kind of person I am, so I'm not going to take offense at what you just said. But I'm telling you this now, completely sober and with every moral fiber in my body. We will be in this together, and any decisions that need to be made will be made by both of us."

Kylie wasn't sure if that was a threat or a vow. He seemed to have an abundance of moral fibers floating around in his perfectly formed body. Yet, behind the clear lenses, his eyes were very serious and solemn. For some reason, his words soothed her, and she no longer felt as though she was drowning alone. The fact remained, though, that she was still drowning. All she could hope was that this guy didn't sink her in his quest to save himself first.

It must've been the lingering effects of the alcohol causing her palms to sweat and her tummy to swirl. Out of all the men she'd gone out with, not once had one's nearness ever made her feel this light-headed.

Kylie needed some food to ease her roiling stomach, and they had only about ten minutes to get to brunch downstairs before their dual absence caused speculation.

"Okay," she said. "Let's agree to get through today and this upcoming week back in Sugar Falls as if nothing has happened." Hopefully, by then, she'd have some more answers—like whether she'd need to buy a pregnancy test and when he'd be on his way out of town and out of her life. "We won't make any decisions until after the wedding. *Their* wedding, that is. Maxine and Cooper's. Not yours and mine. Ugh. You know what I mean."

Great. How was she ever going to get through this brunch if she couldn't even get through a sentence?

"That sounds like a good plan." He stood back up, his hand that had gently stroked her chin now extended in a handshake. She hadn't noticed before but his right pinkie was slightly bent—an interesting flaw in an otherwise perfect specimen of man.

He had replaced an intimate gesture with a business-like stance. So she rose from the chair in order to cover up the fact that she was leaning toward him like a lost kitten seeking out a friendly pat. Had she been wearing her usual four-inch heels, she would have come close to matching his impressive height. However, in her bare feet and over-size robe, she felt more delicate and womanly than she was used to when around average-size men.

Whoa, he was well built. As his hand shook hers, she smiled, thinking that under his preppy sweater and starched jeans was a rippling specimen of a man that only she was privy to. She liked knowing that.

He still hadn't released her from his grip when two

abrupt knocks sounded at the door. Drew turned to answer it and she grabbed his forearm and pulled him back. What was he thinking?

She put a finger to her mouth and shoved him toward the bathroom. A second passed before his brows lifted in surprise. He finally figured out that she wanted to hide him from whoever was knocking. The guy was obviously not schooled in the art of clandestine operations, which was probably a point in his favor. Just not at that exact moment.

She waited until the bathroom knob clicked before opening the hotel room door.

Her best friend's former mother-in-law, Cessy Walker, and Freckles, the owner of the Cowgirl Up Café back home, brushed past her and into what Kylie was sure they would sense was her den of iniquity.

"Are we supposed to meet here for the brunch?" Cessy asked.

"Uh, no." Kylie turned quickly, hoping the women wouldn't notice the remains of last night's debauchery that still littered the nightstand and floor. "We were supposed to meet downstairs at the buffet."

Kylie's frantic search zeroed in on the wedding photo and license she'd left on the chair, and she quickly sat on top of them.

"You're not ready," Cessy said, pointing out the obvious.

"No, I'm running a little late, Mrs. Walker. Why don't you two ladies go on down and let everyone know that we're... I mean, that I'm on my way."

"Kylie." Cessy tsked, looking around the room. "You're one of the maids of honor. You're supposed to be hosting the brunch. It's in bad taste to show up late to your own event."

Hopefully, Sugar Falls's resident society matron wouldn't find out what other forms of bad taste Kylie had recently been engaged in.

"Is your shower running?" asked Freckles—who looked older than Kylie's grandmother, yet dressed as though she was a runner-up in a Dolly Parton lookalike contest.

"Oh. Uh, yeah. I was just about to hop in when you guys knocked."

"Well, we'll just wait out here for you, then. Maybe it'll speed you along."

Kylie thought about the man inside her bathroom who, right this second, was probably lathering up his well-muscled body. She couldn't go in there now or she'd see him in all his angelic glory. She would have blushed in mortification at her lustful thoughts for a stranger, but she was too busy flushing bright red at the realization that the two women looked like they were going to settle in and wait for her to do just that.

Before she could muster a protest, an undoubtedly manly shout sounded from the other side of the door. "Ow! Man, that's slippery!"

Freckles's face split into an ear-to-ear lipstick-covered grin. But her slightly younger and overcontrolling cohort looked confused.

"Who was that?" Cessy asked.

"That's what I call the evidence of a good bachelorette party." Freckles giggled, slapping her painted on jeans–clad thigh.

"Kylie Chatterson, I can't believe you brought a man back to your hotel room—and of all times. You couldn't go one weekend without one?" Cessy looked more exasperated than surprised, and Kylie's pride stung at the implication that promiscuous behavior was expected from her. Normally she would've launched a full verbal attack against any petty remarks directed at her or her loved ones. But the truth of the situation and her growing shame wouldn't allow her to defend her questionable honor.

"Stop being such a prude, Cessy," the other woman said. If Kylie hadn't been sitting across the room in the chair, refusing to budge for fear of revealing the condemning documents, the older waitress probably would've high-fived her.

Freckles was the liberal yin to Cessy's conservative and proper yang. They were a mismatched set of friends, and right about now Kylie fought back tears at their intrusive assumptions. But at this second, she couldn't argue with the evidence. So she bit her lip and tried to come up with a plan to get them out of her room.

"Well, you'd better not bring some one-night stand to my daughter-in-law's prewedding brunch. Cooper's friend, that sweetheart of a man who's performing the wedding, is going to be there. His father is a minister, and Drew himself is a well-respected and high-ranking officer. The last thing we need is for him to think the bride's best friend is hooking up with random men."

The sharp insult was a stiletto to Kylie's heart. She wanted to scream that the almighty, holier-than-thou Doctor Gregson was too busy being naked in her shower and recovering from a hangover of epic proportions to worry about anyone else's misconduct.

But she wouldn't turn this into a bigger scandal and out the poor guy like that—even if misery *did* love company.

Kylie counted to one hundred under her breath. The only thing stopping her from verbally putting Cessy Walker in her place was the fact that, in this situation, Kylie's behavior was indefensible. Even if it seemed to be what everyone anticipated. And that was what hurt the most.

Sure, Kylie wore clothes that were arguably a bit too

sexy by Sugar Falls, Idaho, standards. But underneath the beauty-queen smile, the spandex and the heels, she was a well-balanced and professional woman.

Heck, Kylie even did Cessy Walker's—as well as half the town's—income taxes. It seemed everyone trusted her sensible side when it came to important things like their finances and life savings. But nobody seemed to trust her when it came to moral values that were none of their business anyway.

She was just about to say as much when Freckles finally spoke up and pulled her friend's arm. "Cessy Walker, don't try to shame the girl for having a little fun. You were on your third marriage by the time you were Kylie's age. C'mon now, let's go meet everyone downstairs. She's a big girl and can make her own decisions. Besides, she's so smart…"

Their voices drifted down the hallway as Kylie slammed the door closed.

Just then, Drew poked his head out of the bathroom, probably making sure the coast was clear. "I, uh, don't have any of my clothes except the ones I wore yesterday. Do you think I have time to go back to my room to change?"

His slim hips were barely covered by a knotted white towel; his wide shoulders and tapering torso were too much for her overcrowded mind to take in. "Just put on the same stuff and get down there before me. Nobody will notice what you're wearing anyway."

"Listen," he started, and she could already see the pity in his face. "I couldn't help but hear Mrs. Walker's voice. I'm sorry for the way she spoke to you. I'm sure that if we put our heads together, we can figure out how to minimize the gossip."

His words stung her pride even more than she'd thought possible. She hated anyone feeling sorry for her and was mortified that he'd overheard the older woman chastising her. Her parents had raised her to be tough, and she'd been on the receiving end of worse insults than the ones he'd just overheard. What she couldn't handle was pity. His sympathy implied she had no control over her life and needed Doctor Goodbody to step in and save her.

"Don't worry about it. If there's one thing I've learned, it's that gossip in small towns is pretty standard. So just as long as nobody finds out *who* the man in my room is, I can live with one more blemish on my unearned reputation."

With that, she grabbed his discarded clothes off the bathroom counter and tossed them toward him before locking herself inside. She didn't wait to make sure he left before getting under the hot spray of the shower nozzle to scrub away her sins—along with her hurt and embarrassment. All she wanted was for him to get dressed as quickly as possible and get out of her room before she did something stupid, like let him hold her while she cried her fool eyes out.

But twenty minutes later, when she pageant-walked into the reserved dining room for the prewedding brunch as though everything in her life was as grand as could be, she realized she had seriously underestimated her friends' skills of observation.

After Drew had gone through the buffet line, loading his plate with a custom-made omelet, sausage links and four buttermilk pancakes, he'd tried to sit next to Kylie. He didn't want to seem as if he was avoiding her and, truthfully, he liked being near her. But his best friend and the groom, Matt Cooper, had steered him toward the opposite end of the table.

"You must've gotten lost last night," Cooper said right

before digging into his own breakfast. "Nobody could find you after we left the cocktail lounge."

"Hmm," Drew replied noncommittally as he forked piping-hot eggs into his mouth. He wasn't going to lie to anyone—especially not to Cooper, who was a former military police sergeant and had just been appointed as the chief of police for the town of Sugar Falls. His friend was too canny for that. And, judging from the smug grin across the guy's face, he was also too excited at the prospect of exploiting Drew's possible fall from grace.

"And it looks as though the airlines must have lost your luggage, because you're wearing the exact same clothes you had on when we saw you last."

Yep, the cop definitely knew something had happened. But as much as Drew wanted to confide in his friend, he'd promised Kylie that they wouldn't tell anybody yet. Instead, he shoved a bite of a syrup-drenched pancake into his mouth, trying to avoid answering any more questions.

Drew stole a look down the long table to see how his wife was faring.

Wife.

That sounded weird. Not horrible and scary, he thought. Just weird.

She was seated next to the bride and their friend Mia, the other maid of honor. But unlike Drew, Kylie merely pushed the food back and forth on her plate while her friends talked incessantly around her. She was several feet away from him, but he could've sworn he heard her asking the waitress if the soft-serve ice cream machine was working this early in the day.

"So are you excited about the wedding?" Drew asked Cooper, trying to change the subject. But his buddy wasn't having it.

"Kylie's being rather quiet this morning," Cooper said. "That's kind of unusual for her."

"I wouldn't know. I don't know your friends very well."

"Really? Because you two were thick as thieves last night. I got the feeling you and Kylie were getting to know each other really well."

Drew gave Cooper his listening expression but still didn't respond. He found it was the best way to get information out of people. Unfortunately, Cooper was making the same face.

"Here's the deal," Drew finally relented. "I don't remember much about last night, and I wasn't really myself. So let's just drop it, okay?"

His friend let out a guffaw before patting him on the back. "Don't worry, Saint Drew. Your secret's safe with me. Besides, you could've done a lot worse than Kylie."

"What does that mean?"

"It means that whatever is between you and my soon-to-be wife's best friend is just that—between you two. But I'm still gonna give you a hard time whenever I can."

"Yeah, you're an emotional vault, so I know I can count on you for discretion. You don't talk to anyone about anything." Sadly, Drew was serious, but he knew that since Cooper had met Maxine, his former-loner friend was starting to open up more. "But what do you mean that I could do worse than Kylie? Like I said, I really don't know anything about her."

"Kylie's a good person." Coming from Coop, who was suspicious of everyone, that was quite a compliment. "She's smart as hell and she speaks her mind. Very loyal and protective when it comes to the people she loves. So she dresses a little over-the-top and likes to go out with a new guy every week, but Maxine says she just does that because she was the only girl growing up in a male-dominated household and likes to flaunt her femininity. She's a real spitfire, but she has a heart of gold."

Drew chugged his orange juice, trying not to look at Kylie again. Cooper's assessment pretty much aligned with his own first impression of the woman. At least, what he could remember about it.

"And from the way she's sitting down there all prim and proper, trying not to stare at you just as hard as you're trying not to stare at her, I'd say something good definitely happened between you two."

"And I'd say don't make any risky bets before you leave the casino today. Gambling on the odds isn't in your best interests."

Cooper laughed again, this time drawing the looks of the other twenty or so people crowded around the table.

Drew turned the unwanted attention to his advantage and suddenly announced to the group, "I hate to eat and run, but I'm supposed to be in Boise later today to pick up my nephews. I'll see all of you in Sugar Falls in a few days for the big weekend."

He then excused himself and made his way down the table, saying his goodbyes and shaking hands before he got to the person he wanted to talk to the most.

"Ladies," Drew started, acknowledging both her and her friends, yet Kylie wouldn't look at him or meet his gaze. She kept shoveling ice cream into her mouth so quickly she would no doubt give herself brain freeze. He wanted to get her phone number or figure out a way for them to contact each other since they still had a lot to talk about.

"Drew," Maxine Walker said, looking between him and her redheaded friend. "We'll have to get together as soon as you arrive in Sugar Falls. Cooper tells me you're bringing your nephews with you and staying at the cabin for the summer."

"What?" Kylie's spoon clattered to the floor. "You're moving to Sugar Falls?"

The suspicion in her eyes made him think she was seriously opposed to the news.

"That's the plan." One he didn't intend to change just because he'd stepped out of character one night and had too much to drink.

"Drew's from Boise originally," Maxine explained, probably trying to diffuse her friend's growing tension. "He just transferred assignments and is going to be the psychologist in charge of the new PTSD unit at Shadowview Military Hospital."

"But Shadowview is closer to Boise than to Sugar Falls." What was Kylie getting at? That she would rather him live an hour away so she wouldn't have to be reminded of him or what they'd done?

"Seriously, Kylie," their friend Mia spoke up, a quiet and calm voice of reason. "The hospital is only thirty minutes from the cabin."

"What cabin?" Kylie asked.

"You know, the one off Sweetwater Bend? Where Cooper lived when he first moved to town?" Drew just stood there awkwardly, letting Cooper's fiancée explain everything he should have told Kylie last night. "It belongs to Drew's family. He's going to be living there with his nephews and taking care of them while his brother is on deployment."

"I had absolutely no idea." Kylie wouldn't make eye contact with him, and he decided to get this conversation under control before the woman he'd spent the night with made it obvious to everyone at the table that there was a reason she was acting so uncomfortable around him.

"Kylie, I wanted to talk to you about the wedding rehearsal before I left. Ladies, would you excuse us for just a moment?" He pulled her chair back before she could decline, leaving her no polite choice but to walk away from the table with him.

He hated to coerce her verbally, especially when she'd thrown herself on that little gossip grenade in front of Cessy Walker and Freckles. The only person who had ever covered for him in a potentially disastrous situation like that was his brother, Luke. But he couldn't just sit back and let her martyr herself—or her reputation—without providing his input.

She was just as haughty in her strapless floral-printed sundress as she'd been in her bedsheet this morning. But this time, when she turned to stand toe-to-toe with him, she was almost at eye level. He glanced down at her four-inch wedge-heeled sandals and decided that as regally annoyed as she looked right this second, he liked her similar height to his. As well as her long, toned legs, which made him think thoughts he had no business thinking.

"You never said anything about moving to Sugar Falls," she said accusingly, the sound of slot machines ringing in the background.

"I didn't realize I needed your permission to do so." He tried to keep his voice calm and steady. They were far away from the prying eyes and ears of their acquaintances back at the table, and nobody would be the wiser if they made a scene in the middle of the buffet area. But he knew that if he kept his cool, she would be forced to, as well.

"Of course you don't need my permission. But can't you realize how much more awkward this situation is going to be if we have to live in the same town?"

"Not if we don't *let* things get awkward."

"Maybe you have ice running through your veins, but

I can't run around pretending this—" she held up her ring finger between the two of them "—didn't happen." She must not have been able to get her band off, but she'd camouflaged it by wearing a large ruby-studded one stacked on top. He'd used so much soap in the shower, he'd almost dropped his own down the drain. He reached into his left pocket, just as he'd done several times throughout the meal, making sure it was safely tucked away.

Looking at her bare shoulders and feeling the warm metal circle under his fingers, he knew he had anything but ice coursing through him right that second. In fact, he was almost as heated as he'd been earlier this morning when she stood in front of him in the same stance, all fired up and practically heaving out of her provocative lace bra.

"I think I'm not saying this right." He slowed down his words, hoping this would slow his pulse rate, as well. "We have no idea what we're going to have to deal with in the future, and it would probably help if we could keep things friendly."

"Why are you always so rational?" She sounded as if she was accusing him of something again. Was she seriously expecting an answer? She let out a pent-up breath and then asked a more logical question. "So you're going to be living at that cabin with a couple of kids?"

"Yes."

"But it's only for the summer?"

"Correct. That should give us enough time to know what we're going to do about…uh…everything," he said as he looked pointedly at her midsection. "In the meantime, I wanted to get your number so I could—"

She interrupted him. "Why don't you give me yours instead? I never give my personal number out to strangers. Besides, I'll let you know if there's any news."

Wow. Talk about putting him in his place. Plus she apparently deemed him one who shouldn't get a say in what happened from here on out. He didn't like not being the one in control. Of course, it wasn't as though he couldn't find her if he wanted to. They had the same friends—one of them being the chief of police, who could locate anyone—and Sugar Falls was a small town.

"Okay, let me grab a piece of paper to write it down for you."

"I don't need it. I've got a head for numbers."

He rattled it off, and she repeated it back to him from memory. Impressive.

Now, if only her clever mind could tell him what they'd done last night…

Drew hadn't been able to stop thinking about Kylie the entire flight from Reno to Boise. He had taken a cab from the airport to his parents' house, planning to spend a night or two with his folks so the kids could get reacquainted with him before they left for their summer excursion.

He and Luke had been extraordinarily close growing up and had even joined the navy together when they'd turned eighteen. But their careers had taken opposite paths, and due to the transient nature of their assignments, they rarely saw each other. Which meant Drew saw his nephews even less.

Normally his mom and dad—or even their younger sister—would take the eight-year-old twins whenever Luke was sent overseas for an indefinite length of time. But Hannah was participating in a Teachers Without Borders program this summer, and his parents were getting a little too advanced in years to handle the high-energy boys. Besides, it was time Drew stepped in for some family bonding, especially when he finally had a duty station that wasn't in a war zone.

But after twenty minutes in the house with the wild and rambunctious kids, he wondered if he was equipped to handle so much rowdiness all by himself.

"Uncle Drew," Aiden called out as he stood on the armrest of the sofa. "You look just like Dad, but with hair."

"You look just like Caden, but with mustard on your face," Drew responded. "And get down from there."

"*I'm* Caden," Aiden tried to insist. But Drew was an identical twin himself and knew the old trick.

"Does the switcheroo work on your dad?" Drew doubted it did, and it was best that the boys learn right away that he was going to be just as effective at parenting as his brother. Of course, judging by the complete lack of discipline he'd witnessed so far, he didn't think the boys had been exposed to *any* effective parenting, no matter how much Luke adored his children.

"Not when he's here. But when we Skype him, we can usually fool him good. And we fool Grammie all the time."

"Well, Grammie should know better. After all, nobody's better at the twin switch than me and your old man."

At that moment, Caden ran by, shoving a brownie into his mouth as Drew's mom chased him, a rubber spatula in her hand. "Aiden Andrew Gregson, you bring that brownie back right this minute."

"Grammie, that's Caden. I'm Aiden." The boy who'd been talking to Drew giggled, still balancing on the furniture like a tightrope walker. "See? She mixes us up all the time."

"Well, it doesn't help that your names are almost identical, too. It can be confusing for anyone." Drew lifted Aiden up before planting the boy's sturdy legs on the floor. What had their parents been thinking, naming them so similarly?

But he didn't ask this out loud because he wasn't sure how the kids were reacting to their father's recent deployment. Their mother had passed away when the boys were three, and Luke had raised them mostly on his own when he wasn't playing Captain Save-the-World. Yet the past couple of years, they had bounced around so much to accommodate their dad's dangerous and unpredictable job in special ops, they hadn't had much consistency.

"Aiden, give me back that spatula," Drew's mom yelled, as she chased Caden and his chocolate-covered face back through the living room. She'd now lost her spatula and all control.

"Grammie can never catch us. We're way too fast for her," Aiden boasted.

"Caden," he called out, and the running boy suddenly halted. Drew wasn't a voice raiser and wasn't about to start now. Why yell when you could rationally explain your position? Of course, he doubted that his normal communication tools would be as effective with these two.

Plus, he was still somewhat of a novelty, so the boys were sizing him up. He motioned both of the children over to him and knelt down so he didn't tower over them. His brother had the same build, so he knew they wouldn't be intimidated by his size. But he wanted to be on eye level with them so they would be forced to look at him to hear what he had to say.

"You two are going to go wash up and get your pajamas on."

"We don't want to take no baths," Caden whined as Aiden dropped to the floor in a dramatic heap.

"Your dad and I didn't like taking baths when we were your age, either. But we weren't allowed to have brownies or play Robot Blasters unless we were clean."

"What are Robot Blasters?" Aiden hopped up to attention, his despair quickly turning to eagerness.

"It's a special game only for twins. Your dad and I made

it up a long time ago, and it's very secret and unique. I can't tell you about it until you can show that you're able to follow rules and directions."

"I call front bath." Caden ran off to be first in the bathroom, Aiden hurrying to catch up.

"I hate getting stuck in the stern," his brother complained, but he followed anyway.

Drew's mom collapsed on the sofa, clearly winded after her brownie-turned-spatula chase. "I can't keep up with them like I used to."

"Where's Dad?" Drew asked.

"He's at the health club, doing his water therapy. He's been staying away more this visit. Says his sciatica has been acting up. But I think he's just suffering from a case of naughty twinitis."

His folks had been great parents, involved in everything from the Little League to the Cub Scouts. Marty Gregson had been a youth pastor when he'd met his wife, Donna, a schoolteacher. They'd both had a natural love for children, which Drew's sister had inherited. But they were at the start of their golden years. And plainly, his unruly nephews were more than their retired lives could handle.

"I swear I love those boys to death, and so does your father. But I can't tell you how grateful we are that you're pulling a shift this summer. In fact, Dad didn't want me to tell you this, but we've already got the RV loaded up, and the minute you drive off with the kids, we're leaving for our grand tour. I thought it only fair to warn you that by the time you make it to the cabin, there won't be the opportunity for any take-backs." She must have seen his horrified expression. "I'm kidding, of course. We'll be a phone call away if you need anything. You guys will be fine."

Drew plopped down beside her, not sure if he was ready for the biggest responsibility he'd yet to face. He really needed her to tell him there would be light at the end of this tunnel. "It's only three months, right?"

"I know you can do it, honey. Sure, they're a handful, but you're a trained psychologist. You're used to dealing with behavior outside the norm, right?"

"Mom, I work with soldiers, not children."

"Drew, it's about time you settled down. You have a wonderful opportunity to spend time with your nephews and give this whole domesticity thing a try. It's time to stop analyzing everything from behind all those textbooks of yours and start actually living life. Of course, it'd probably be easier if you were married and had an extra set of hands to help you, but your brother does this on his own all the time."

Drew thought about Kylie and how, if they were married in the true sense of the word, she'd be helping him. Man, she might be helping him anyway if it turned out that she was pregnant. He didn't even know if the woman liked kids. Or wanted them.

He was pretty sure *he* did, but then he looked toward the open bathroom door and saw the soaking wet hallway carpet. Before he could ask his mom about a flooding problem or a possible burst pipe, Donna Gregson shot off the sofa, her bare feet squishing with each running step on the flooded rug.

"Boys, I told you no more playing battleship or hurricane watch in the bathtub."

A child's squeal was followed by the crashing sound of water.

"That's it. I'm going to bed." His mom retreated, completely drenched from what Drew assumed was a water attack. "You're on duty for now, Lieutenant Commander. Your father should be home in an hour if you need reinforcements." She sloshed her way down to the end of the hall, and he heard the lock on the master bedroom door click into place.

After the morning he'd had, he'd promised himself he'd never drink again. But being confronted with two unmanageable nephews—and who knew what other problems awaiting him with Kylie in Sugar Falls—it took several minutes of mindful meditation and an unearthly amount of willpower to head to the linen closet for a stack of towels instead of running directly to his parents' liquor cabinet.

Chapter Three

Kylie hadn't called him once since they'd seen each other in Reno. And this past week, Drew had been so deep in the exploits of a couple of eight-year-olds, he didn't know when he'd find a chance to seek her out now that he was officially in Sugar Falls.

Caden and Aiden had helped to take his mind off the situation, but only because they kept up a steady pace of disobedience and messes, leaving no downtime between their wrestling matches, arguments, food fights and predilections to log onto his laptop to access online video games rated for mature users.

The increasing need to keep them under constant supervision took every ounce of mental energy Drew possessed. At this rate, he didn't know how he'd make it through this weekend, let alone this summer. He enrolled the boys in a local day-camp program starting on Monday, but he feared he'd barely get to the base hospital to report for duty before getting a call advising him that the twins were being kicked out.

He peered at his reflection in the small mirror in the cabin's single bathroom. The man staring back at him looked as though he'd been on a battlefield. And after his last few deployments, he knew he wasn't exaggerating. There was a reason he specialized in PTSD and not in child psychology.

He heard the boys getting restless in the living room and, if he wanted them to not look like complete ruffians before they got to the wedding rehearsal, he needed to get out there quickly while their clothes were still somewhat dirt- and chocolate-free.

According to his mother—who hesitated to disclose her and his dad's travel itinerary for fear Drew would give up too quickly and load up the boys to track them down in their motor home—his nephews had been kicked out of several after-school clubs, piano classes and swim lessons and two city libraries. Their school had threatened expulsion last year, but Luke had stepped in and sweet-talked the single schoolteacher into giving them another chance.

Drew wondered if his brother had ever considered sending the eight-year-olds away to military school. Or to one of those scared-straight prison programs. As it was, the only time Drew was able to let down his guard was when they were both wearing their life vests and bike helmets. At the same time.

Thank goodness he'd finally get to see Kylie tonight. He was anxious to know how she was dealing with everything and if she'd made any decisions. He was also desperate for a little adult company and for the boys to meet some other children their own age.

Maxine's eleven-year-old son, Hunter, would be there, and hopefully, the older boy could take Caden and Aiden under his wing. Or at least peer-pressure them into acting like semicivilized human beings.

Drew wrestled the kids into their seat belts and drove toward Snow Creek Lodge, where the wedding would be held tomorrow. The nonstop talking from the backseat didn't keep him from thinking of what he'd say to Kylie when he saw her. Or how she'd look.

The minute they arrived and he put his borrowed car in Park, the two chatterboxes bolted out of the backseat and ran straight for the ski lift—which, during the summer, was used to haul mountain cyclists and their bikes up to the top of the peak.

"Boys," he said when he finally caught up to them and forcibly steered them away from the moving benches. "Remember, no candy bars later if you act up while we're here." Drew hated using sweets as a bribe, but tonight was important, and he couldn't have them misbehaving.

The boys, going on their third day with no sugar since they'd yet to behave well enough to earn the coveted prize, finally fell into step—one on each side of him. The trio walked into the oversize log structure and, before he could blink, the twins took off toward a small group of boys huddled around their handheld electronic devices.

Aiden and Caden could sniff out video-game systems within a ten-mile radius. They were like arcade bloodhounds. Originally, Drew had planned to introduce them to everyone, but why ruin a good thing? They should be safe enough over there with their attention focused for a solid thirty minutes at least. And it might keep them out of trouble.

Maybe.

"There's the man in charge," Cooper, still wearing his uniform, called out as he walked toward him. Everyone else in the wedding party turned in their direction, and he found himself eagerly searching out the one woman he'd been waiting all week to see.

"Is everyone here and ready to get started?" Even as Drew asked the question, he could see that she wasn't there.

He shoved his hands into his pockets, feeling the band he'd been carrying in the left one. Was she purposely avoiding him?

"Kylie's running late," Maxine said. "But don't worry. She's been in so many weddings, she could do this in her sleep."

Or with a drunk stranger in Reno.

"Okay, well, then, let's begin." Drew directed everyone on how to walk down the aisle, where to stand and what to say. He couldn't believe this was the way Cooper was making him repay the pen pal favor and he actually had to perform this ceremony. Unlike the absent redhead, he was no wedding expert. But he was a researcher and a perfectionist and had studied enough online videos lately to get through this rehearsal blindfolded.

Maxine's son, Hunter, handed over his PlayStation to the twins so that he could walk his mother down the aisle. But the boys, both overly eager to take their turn at playing, fought over the small device, each one grappling and scratching to get control of the coveted possession.

Drew was about to head toward his nephews to break up the fight, but Kylie strode into the room at that exact moment, confident and oblivious to the childish skirmish going on nearby. When he saw her, he froze, waiting for her to see him.

She looked poised and completely unflustered—until she glanced in his direction. Her smile faltered, but otherwise, she gave no outward sign that she was uncomfortable in his presence. She also gave no sign that she was going to slow her stride long enough to talk with him.

Which was unfortunate, because if she had, the small video game console that had just been launched into the air wouldn't have hit her right in the face.

"Ouch!" she yelled, her hand flying to her right eye. "What in the hell was that?"

Caden, who wasn't used to hearing adults swear, began giggling, while Aiden made a fast getaway toward the restroom—probably to escape the pending chaos he'd helped cause.

All of the women ran toward their startled friend, asking if she was okay and trying to soothe her. The men went in the direction of the children, breaking up the video game party, while Hunter ran to his toy, which had landed with a pop and then immediately suffered the wrath of Kylie's spiked heel when she'd blindly stepped on it.

"My new game is totally broken!" Hunter cried.

Drew grabbed Caden by the shoulder and marched him toward the restroom, where he'd seen the boy's brother run for cover.

The twins had yet to see Uncle Drew at his boiling point. Really, nobody had seen the calm counselor lose his cool in quite a few years, but the two eight-year-olds were about to get a peek at what he'd successfully held under wraps for so long.

"You guys not only broke Hunter's game but also seriously hurt that poor woman out there. And all because you were fighting over whose turn it was. You've both been acting selfish and wild since I picked you up from Grammie and Pop's, and I refuse to allow things to continue like this."

Drew was livid and the boys finally looked remorseful.

"Are you gonna send us away to live with someone

else, Uncle Drew?" Aiden had fat tears trickling down his chubby cheeks.

The emotional pressure had been building all week and, with the combined stress of the Kylie situation, Drew was at his wit's end.

In the bathroom mirror, he caught sight of the vein pulsing along the right side of his neck. He took a deep breath, trying to come up with the best way to take control of this derailed mess.

"Nobody'll take us." Caden stared at his scruffy sneakers, refusing to meet his uncle's eyes. "Nobody wants us."

"Why would you think something like that?" asked Drew.

"'Cause Dad is always going off on assignments and Grammie and Pop said their new motor home isn't kid-proofed yet and wouldn't take us on vacation with them."

"Guys." Drew tried to find the ideal thing to say to ease Caden's fear, but the perfect words were escaping him. "Just because they're not here doesn't mean they don't want to be with you."

"Yeah, right," said Aiden, sniffing back a tear of his own. "Even Aunt Hannah ditched us."

What did Drew's sister have to do with this? "Aunt Hannah is doing important work teaching at an orphanage."

"So? Me and Caden are practically orphans. Why'd she have to go all the way to Africa for that unless she was trying to get away from us, too?"

The throbbing in Drew's neck lowered to his heart and became more of a dull ache. His poor nephews were dealing with something bigger than just a lack of discipline. He sighed before easing himself to the tile floor. "Listen, boys. You are not orphans. You have a big, wonderful family that cares so much about you. And nobody ditched you guys. It was my turn to get a chance finally to spend some time with you because I love you and I want you. But you guys have to love me, too. I need you to start acting as if you *want* to be with me. When you misbehave and don't follow the rules, it tells me that you don't respect me and that you're not happy being with me."

"But we *do* like to be with you." Aiden was still sniffling, but at least the tears had subsided.

"Then, you guys need to show me. I want us to have a fun summer, but we need to work together as a team, okay?"

"Okay," the boys agreed and Drew pulled them in, making it a three-way embrace.

"Good. Now you're going to go out there and apologize to the nice lady who got hit in the face. And then you're going to apologize to Hunter for breaking his video game. After that, you're going to behave for the rest of the night. Starting tomorrow, both of you will do chores around the cabin to earn enough money to pay for a new system to replace the one that broke. Got it?"

Both boys nodded, but neither one looked happy about their future plans. Frankly, thinking of the injured woman out there and her refusal to call him all week, Drew wasn't feeling too optimistic, either.

He escorted the twins back outside and, seeing that Kylie and several of the women were no longer there, he walked his nephews over to Hunter, who was still cradling the broken PlayStation in his hands.

"We're sorry for breaking your video game." Caden was the first to apologize, and Drew had to nudge the other boy to follow suit.

"Yeah. I'm sorry my brother wouldn't let me finish my turn and grabbed it out of my hands." Aiden, the one who'd been the most sorrowful looking, was now the one acting the least remorseful.

Just as the boys began to argue about who should be more sorry, Chief Cooper knelt down to talk with them. As he did, the former marine and current police chief reached into the back pouch on his utility belt and pulled out a pair of stainless-steel handcuffs. He snapped the cuffs open and closed as he spoke quietly to the boys.

As far as scare tactics went, his buddy's methods were effective. Cooper definitely had the twins' attention. And since his friend seemed to have everything under control, Drew decided to seek out the woman he'd wanted to talk to for the past five days.

She was coming out of the ladies' room, a linen napkin–covered bag of ice over her right eye. Damn—that looked bad.

"Kylie." Drew started toward her. "I'm so sorry. They were overexcited and haven't had a lot of discipline and, well, there's no excuse for what they did."

"Drew, it was an accident. It wasn't as if they threw that thing at me on purpose." As soon as the words were out of her mouth, but before he could talk to her about everything else that needed saying, the boys ran up, stumbling over their own apologies.

Drew was glad that both of them seemed sincere in their contrition. His nephews might be wild, but they weren't malicious.

"Wow, does that hurt?" Caden asked when Kylie lowered the ice pack and revealed the bruise that was already turning a deep shade of purple around her eye.

She knelt down to talk to them, and Aiden reached out his finger to touch her bruise. But Kylie's reflexes—even with only one functioning eye—were quicker. "It only hurts when something touches it."

"Well, we really are sorry," Aiden said sincerely.

"We're gonna do chores to earn money to pay for

Hunter to get a new video game," Caden added. "And Chief Cooper said he would put us to work at the police station so maybe we can make enough to pay for you to go see a doctor. Uncle Drew is a doctor and starts work at the hospital soon, so he can take you with him if you need a shot or anything."

"Thank you, boys, but I don't think I need to see a doctor or get a shot just yet. And I forgive you as long as next time you promise to try to do a better job of sharing."

"We will," they chorused.

Drew didn't realize he'd been holding his breath, waiting for her to yell at the kids. Even though they deserved a scathing reprimand, he was glad to see she was giving them grace instead.

"Now," she said, standing and tossing her ice pack on a nearby table before taking both boys by the hand. "I have a very important job for both of you." She walked with them outside and toward the grassy area where the ceremony would be held.

As Drew watched her leading his nephews around, talking to them as if she didn't think they were little monsters at all, he was overwhelmed with appreciation. She was being more than forgiving, considering the fact that by this time tomorrow, she'd be sporting a shiner of epic proportions.

If he could convince her that the twins weren't so terrible, maybe he could convince her that he wasn't the type of person who usually acted so recklessly with women. Not that he should have to prove himself, but if he was going to be living in Sugar Falls for the summer, it would be nice to know a friendly—and beautiful—face. Besides, he needed all the help he could get, and Kylie seemed to have a talent for reining in the boys. Which gave him an idea...

* * *

Kylie wasn't one for praying, but the following morning she almost dropped to her knees to give thanks—right there in a bathroom stall at the Snow Creek Lodge. Finally, ten minutes before her best friend's wedding ceremony, she got her period.

Hallelujah!

She'd thought about Drew almost every minute since he'd left Reno on Sunday, and she was desperate to talk to him. To find out how he felt about everything. To have him reassure her that their crazy night together wasn't going to ruin both of their lives.

But every time she'd dialed his number, she'd been too embarrassed to push the Send button. Normally when she was under stress, she'd immerse herself in hot-fudge sundaes and her work. She had no scientific proof, but for some reason, ice cream helped to chill out her fiery temper. And working with numbers made sense to her—they soothed her and forced her mind to think logically. She liked their dependability and the fact that she could always count on one plus one equaling two.

Yet by yesterday morning, after she'd recalculated the same column of figures three times and was too embarrassed to make a second trip into Noodie's Ice Cream Shoppe in town, she finally blew off work to go shopping. She drove straight to downtown Boise for some retail therapy in order to get her mind off the knowledge that later in the evening, she'd have to come face-to-face with Drew and what they had done.

She'd bought a new pair of designer jeans that sat low on her hips and fit perfectly. It was usually tough to find an inseam that could accommodate her extensive limbs *and* her high heels. When she'd spotted the pair at her favorite boutique, she'd taken it as a good omen and changed right there in the store.

Amazing how a new outfit could restore the confidence she'd been grasping for all week. In fact, by the time Kylie had grabbed a double-scoop cone at a nearby drugstore, hopped in her convertible Mercedes coupe and hit the country station on satellite radio, she was almost looking forward to seeing Drew again.

Well, maybe not looking forward to it, but at least she wasn't dreading the potential look of disgust—or worse, pity—on his face when he saw her.

Then she'd gotten stuck in a traffic jam coming back up the mountain and was late to the rehearsal. He might have thought she was avoiding him, and the last impression she wanted to give him was that she was hiding in humiliation or that she wasn't woman enough to handle their situation. So when she'd strutted into the Snow Creek Lodge last night, she did so in her sexy new jeans and with her head held high.

Which was probably why she hadn't been paying attention when those little towheaded mischief makers had hit her in the eye with that video game.

Kylie stood and smoothed down her bridesmaid dress— a champagne-colored sheath that Cessy referred to as "unforgiving" when the overbearing woman had seen her take an extra serving of dessert last night—and exited the restroom stall to wash up.

As she looked at her reflection in the mirror, she couldn't help the smile that tugged at the corner of her glossed lips. She was so relieved that she wasn't pregnant and couldn't wait to tell Drew the news. He was officially off the hook. He was no longer under any obligation toward her.

Of course, the makeup artist her friend Mia had hired

hadn't been able to do much with Kylie's black eye, and
she wished that she could've looked her best when she finally did get her chance to talk to the guy.

"Kylie Chatterson, get the lead out," Cessy yelled
through the bathroom door. "Everyone is lining up."

It was time.

Well, not *her* time. Maxine's time. But someday it
would be her time. She'd been a bridesmaid for numerous cousins, sorority sisters and fellow cheerleaders. She
was a pro when it came to walking down the aisle at other
people's weddings.

She let out a breath, then hustled out of the restroom
and took her place in line with the rest of the bridal party.
When the bagpiper launched into Mendelssohn's "Wedding March," Kylie's tummy fluttered and she had to lock
her elbows to keep her small bouquet from trembling.

"You okay, Kylie?" the bride asked from behind her.

"Of course I am. I'm just so excited for you." Her best
friend looked so sweet in a strapless gown a few shades
lighter than the bridesmaids' dresses.

"Your eye doesn't look so horrible today, Aunt Kylie,"
Hunter said. He was giving his mother away, and Kylie
was stunned by how mature he looked.

Where was the time going? People always said that kids
grew up so fast, and she felt a sting of realization that she
might never have kids of her own. Or even find someone
with whom she'd *want* to have kids.

Cessy cued Mia to head out, and Kylie was up next.

What was wrong with her? Two minutes ago she'd been
mentally high-fiving herself in the bathroom for not being
pregnant, and now she was almost despondent over the
fact that she might miss her chance at marriage and moth-
erhood.

It must be hormones putting her on edge. She'd never

been resentful of her always-a-bridesmaid-never-a-bride status, and she certainly hadn't been this anxious any other time she'd been in a bridal party. The truth was, she loved weddings.

Of course, she'd apparently loved them a little *too* much when she was drinking from tacky souvenir cups in Reno.

So if she wasn't nervous, then why was she working prime factorization problems in her mind? She only did that when she...

"And go!" Cessy pushed her through the patio doors, interrupting Kylie midthought.

Suddenly, every number she'd ever stored in her head floated away, and all she could think of was the attractive, tall blond man standing at the end of the aisle. And she didn't mean the groom.

Kylie put one strappy-heeled sandal in front of the other and made her way to him.

There was no golden aura radiating behind the guy, but seeing Drew standing up there in his full military dress uniform, there might as well have been. He was like a beacon of light. When his eyes locked on to hers, she was powerless against the reassuring smile drawing her toward him.

She'd heard of tunnel vision before but had never experienced it until now. She had no idea who was seated to her left or right, and as she walked along the white runner strewn with flower petals, she didn't care. Her nerves were drowning in a sea of emotion, and Drew was the lifeboat she needed to reach.

Why did he have to be so handsome? And so serene? And so damn tall?

For a heartbeat, she almost wished she'd married him on purpose...

Mia, the other maid of honor, had to grab Kylie's elbow

to pull her into position near the floral arch. Next, Maxine and Hunter came down the aisle toward them, but her mind didn't register anything except Drew's presence. She doubted this was how Pistole Pepe and Maddog Molly had felt when she'd walked through the doors at the Silver Rush Wedding Chapel.

She needed to get a grip. Drew was just a man. She was recovering from a stress-filled week. Numbers. Focus on numbers. *The prime factors of nine are three and three. The prime factors of ten are two and five...*

The ceremony began and she was almost to eighty-six when Drew ordered the bride and groom to face each other. Maxine thrust her bouquet at Kylie as Mia straightened the bridal train. While Cooper repeated his vows, Kylie couldn't stop herself from looking at Drew. His blue eyes were staring just as intensely at her, and heat flooded over her skin.

Had they said these same vows to each other? Had he promised to love her and cherish her? And had she promised to stand by him in sickness and in health?

Kylie had romanticized the idea of marriage since childhood. But she'd never understood the sanctity of those solemn vows until that exact moment. Loyalty had been drilled into her since childbirth. Drunk or not, how could she walk away from a promise like that?

How could he?

Drew spoke the rest of the words to formalize their friends' union, but she couldn't help noticing how many times he looked at her when he got to the important bits. Maybe it was subconscious on his part. Or maybe he was serious when he'd told her that he didn't take his promises lightly. She wondered if, once she told him he was off the hook in the daddy department, he wouldn't sweat the whole "oath before God" thing so much.

As Cooper kissed the bride, she shot another look Drew's way and could've sworn that he winked at her.

A burst of fire shot up from inside her chest and through her neck, into her cheeks.

Almost the entire town of Sugar Falls was present today, and he had the audacity to wink at her. In full view and with everyone watching. Oh, the gossip that would be fueled if the town busybodies thought she was flirting with Saint Drew. But before she could speculate about a potential Winkgate, the two little boys who'd graced her with the black eye to end all black eyes last night ran up the aisle to fulfill their job assignments.

"One, two, three, blow," they shouted in unison before releasing a steady stream of bubbles in the air. The audience soon followed suit with the small white bottles Kylie had given the twins to pass out, and the new mister and missus walked down the aisle in a cloud of bubbles.

"You are quite the enchantress," Drew whispered to her as she waited for her turn in the bridal recessional. And her face grew even hotter. "I don't know how you got them to listen to you."

Oh, he was talking about the twins. Not about her seductive appearance. Bummer.

"I had four brothers," she whispered back. "When it comes to little boys, you have to make them feel important and keep them busy. And I bought five gallons' worth of bubbles, so they should be pretty busy for at least another twenty minutes."

"Good," he said right before she departed to the sound of the bagpipes. "Because we still need to talk."

She caught his smile before she walked away, and the nerves zapping around inside her turned to butterflies. He was just as handsome as she remembered. Even more so in his formal navy uniform.

But she wasn't ready to have the overdue discussion yet. She'd been looking for the perfect man for so long, she didn't think that she could handle another failure in her ongoing quest. At least, not publicly.

Man, she needed a pint of Ben & Jerry's if she hoped to get through the upcoming reception.

Instead, she grabbed a glass of champagne from the tray of the first server passing by, wishing it was a root beer float, and tried not to guzzle it down while they posed for pictures after the ceremony.

The terraced garden of the Snow Creek Lodge wasn't that small, but Drew was never far from her sight. Or her mind.

He finally moved in next to her when the photographer took the bride and groom away for some shots by themselves. "Hey."

She'd known this moment was coming, and it was probably best if she got it over with as quickly as possible. Just like pulling off an eyebrow-waxing strip.

"Hi," she said, looking around for another server. Or her sunglasses. Anything that would keep her from meeting his incredible blue eyes.

"You've been pretty good at avoiding me all week." Wow, he wasn't even going to beat around the bush or make small talk. The man definitely said what was on his mind.

Maybe if she could flag down one of the waiters, she could ask him to bring her a milk shake. "I wasn't avoiding you so much as I was trying to figure out how I felt about everything."

"And how do you feel?"

"Confused. Upset. Cheated. Relieved. All of the above."

"Why cheated?"

"I don't know. I guess because like every other girl, I've

always dreamed of the perfect guy and having the fairy-tale wedding. Nowhere in my dreams did I envision marrying some stranger at a tacky wedding chapel in Reno."

"Why relieved?"

"Because I got my…uh…you know…this morning."

"Your what?"

The man was so straitlaced he didn't even get her polite reference. Of course, she was too embarrassed to say it, either. "I'm not pregnant," she whispered.

"Oh." Was it her imagination or did those broad shoulders of his just slump a little? He definitely wasn't smiling. This wasn't exactly the reaction she was expecting. Was he actually disappointed she wasn't having his baby? He must not have understood her.

Yet before she could tell the poor guy that he was off the hook, that they were *both* off the hook, two women approached them.

"Dr. Gregson, that was such a touching service."

Elaine Marconi and her husband owned the local gas station, making her a prime source of neighborhood gossip. The woman was known to overindulge at parties with an open bar, and judging by the flush on her cheeks, today's event was no exception.

The other woman, Marcia Duncan, owned Duncan's Market, another center for all newsworthy information about Sugar Falls.

"I hope you'll be willing to do a guest lecture at our Women in Crafting Crisis meeting while you're in town," Marcia said. "We've never had a licensed psychologist speak with our group."

"Thank you for thinking of me, but I'm a better listener than I am a speaker," the always perfect Drew answered, being perfectly polite. As usual.

Marcia's eyes widened as if her Spanx were cutting off

circulation to her brain, then blinked several times as if to regain her composure.

"But we could really use your professional help," the woman insisted. Kylie knew Marcia ran her market with a strong, meaty fist and probably wasn't used to people telling her no.

"Some more than others," Kylie muttered before looking longingly at the chocolate fountain being set up inside the ballroom.

When Drew smiled at her, acknowledging that he'd heard her impolite comment, her knees wobbled. She remembered how he'd looked in that hotel room, all bare chested and calm, and she almost wished she could be back there again.

"Let me get settled here in town first, ladies. Then we can talk more about it at a later date." Drew's words took the edge off Kylie's snide remark, which she doubted anyone else heard, judging by the way both women looked somewhat appeased.

"Good Lord, Kylie," Elaine suddenly said, as if she'd just now noticed Kylie standing right there. "What in the world happened to your eye? Was it another date gone bad?"

Her hand shot up to the bruise and she silently cursed herself for not grabbing her dark sunglasses when she had the chance. Despite the woman's implication, Kylie didn't date abusive guys.

It had been a rough week, and if Kylie wasn't such a lady, rigorously trained in poise and decorum by some of the best pageant coaches in the nation, she might have been tempted to unleash some violence of her own.

But she was stronger than that. She was better than that. She saw that sympathetic look in Drew's eye again and was briefly tempted to show him she wasn't a woman to be pitied.

"Actually," Drew spoke up, "my twin nephews did that to her. It was an accident." Was it Kylie's imagination or had Drew stepped closer to her? She must have been suffering from some sort of knight-in-shining-armor fantasy because she couldn't help but sense that he was riding to her rescue.

"Oh, I'm sure it was. Are those adorable blond cuties yours?" Marcia turned her back to Kylie, putting her greasy appetizer fingers on Drew's biceps.

"They were just so sweet, blowing all those bubbles," Elaine crooned in a voice that was one glass of chardonnay away from slurring. "You were so smart to come up with the idea for them to do that."

This was Kylie's opportunity to slip away silently, while the ladies were busy slithering up to Saint Drew. But just as she started backing up, Drew's hand shot out and snatched her elbow, pulling her to his side and back into the barracuda-infested waters with him. "Actually, that was Kylie's brilliant idea. She has a way with kids."

Although she was capable of fighting her own battles, Kylie appreciated Drew trying to defuse the situation. But she didn't know if she appreciated the strength of his irontight grip as he held her in place right next to him. Ugh. She knew the guy was made of solid muscle, but she wasn't used to men being strong enough to maneuver her around however they wanted.

"A way with kids?" Marcia's laugh came out as more of a snort.

"Kylie?" Elaine giggled like a teenage girl drunk on her first wine cooler. "Oh, Doctor, she may be good with numbers, but the one thing Kylie does *not* have a way with is kids."

"Or men." Marcia snorted again.

Kylie tried to pull away, but Drew's hand was like velvet-covered steel—deceptively soft on the outside but rigid in its refusal to let go. Her emotions had been on a roller coaster for the past six days, and the last thing she could stomach was standing here and letting these two offensive women insult her in front of the first man she actually liked and respected.

Oh, no. It was true. She actually liked Drew. Even though she knew nothing about him.

Except that he was standing by her side and looking at her with a growing sense of concern. "Now, ladies," he said. "I am under the impression that Kylie here can handle herself in any situation."

Perfect Drew was being his usual calm and diplomatic self. Sure, he probably thought he was protecting her, but he could protect her better by just letting her get the heck away from the reception. Why wouldn't he let go of her arm?

"Oh, we didn't mean anything negative by it." Elaine sobered up enough to stop smirking. Mostly.

"Kylie, honey," Marcia spoke up. "You know we think the world of you. We don't think less of you for dating all those guys or dressing like you do. It must be so hard to be your age and still be single."

"I'm fine," Kylie said through clenched teeth. Maybe Doctor Strong Arms thought he was helping her, but he was really just making things increasingly awkward. Even though her reputation wasn't truly earned, she hated that these harpies made her seem desperate and inadequate in front of Drew, who looked less like a saint right that second and more like a warrior. His eyes darkened to a stormy blue-black, and she could see the pulse in his neck throbbing.

Was he annoyed with Kylie? He couldn't possibly believe what these women were saying about her. Could he?

"Of course you're not fine. Your best friend just got married and you still aren't able to find a man for yourself. We should have been more sensitive."

"Don't stress so much about it, honey. The right man for you is out there somewhere if you would just stop looking so hard. Have you thought about online dating?"

The red haze blinding her eyes and the steam coming out of her ears were making it difficult to tell which woman was saying what. But then a finger brushed along her arm, and the anger broke long enough for her to glance at the man beside her.

We're in this together, Drew mouthed.

She raised her brow, not sure she understood. Her eyes went wide when he snaked his arm around her waist and pull her tighter against his side.

Apparently his annoyance wasn't directed toward her at all.

The women must have taken notice of his intimate and protective stance, because they paused midplatitude, mouths slightly ajar.

Kylie couldn't stop herself from rising to her full five feet ten inches—actually, over six feet in her gold-studded heels—and slid her free hand across Drew's chest, feeling the quickening of his heartbeat.

"Thank you for your concern, ladies, but as you can see," she said, holding out her hand, displaying the tight wedding ring she still couldn't get off and pasting on her best pageant smile, "I don't need your sympathy, because I'm already married."

Chapter Four

What had she just done?

Drew barely managed half a smile at Marcia and Elaine before rushing off behind Kylie as she walked away from the two shocked women in strong, purposeful strides, pulling Drew's hand with her.

He hadn't been expecting her announcement, and now he needed to reconfigure his next course of action.

"How fast do you think word will spread?" he tried to joke as they made their way toward the patio doors. She didn't answer because she was mumbling something about prime numbers and double scoops.

When they were safely inside the cooler air-conditioned ballroom, she finally stopped her numerical chant and let out a deep breath. Thank goodness the guests were still enjoying the cocktail hour outside so that he could be alone with her for a minute. Together, they might be able to figure out how to deal with what they'd just publically acknowledged.

"I'd wager sixty-five percent of the guests here will know by the time we sit down for dinner," she said. "The other thirty-five percent will figure it out when I'm noticeably absent from the bouquet toss. And when you take into account social media, the rest of the town and half of my Boise State graduating class will know by tomorrow morning."

She slumped into a linen-covered chair and propped her elbows on the decorated table before burying her face in her hands. Could being married to him truly cause her this much shame? He pulled his own chair in front of her and sat down facing her.

Well, he would wait her out. She couldn't hide her head forever and pretend nothing had happened. Soon she'd be forced to look at him, once she was done with her pity party, or her multiplication tables, or whatever it was she was doing. But after a few moments, she still hadn't looked up. What was she thinking?

Heck, what was *he* thinking, letting her get sucked into the nest of those two vipers? He'd known the women had been taunting Kylie, and he could tell by the way her arm had been tensing in his grip that she'd been getting frustrated. But instead of being the trained observer, watching her to see how she was going to react, he'd blindly jumped right into the snake pit.

And now the rest of the world was going to know that the naval officer they'd inadvertently designated as some sort of paragon of virtue was married to the town vixen.

At least according to Marcia and Elaine. Fortunately, Drew was a patient man and knew there were two sides to every story.

Apparently, he'd just made it clear that he was choosing her side. Like he'd told her in the hotel room back in Reno, they really were in this together. They needed to figure out a strategy to deal with this new development, stat. And it wouldn't be a bad idea to have some backup support locked into place.

"Perhaps we should go find our friends and tell them the good news before they hear it from everyone else," he suggested.

"Oh, no," she said, finally looking up at him with what could only be described as panic in her eyes. "I mean, yes. We should. And we will. But give me a second to get all my feelings in check. Ugh. I've been a shrink's wife for all of a week and already I'm blowing it. My brothers always teased me for not being able to control my emotions. What have I done?"

There went her face, back into her hands. Where was the Amazon warrior queen he'd seen back in that hotel room and then again outside a few moments ago with those busybodies when she'd flashed her ring in triumph? Kylie didn't strike him as the type to just bury her head in surrender.

"It wasn't just you. I was right there with you and didn't put a stop to it. You haven't done anything that can't be undone. So what if the town finds out about us? They don't need to know the…uh…circumstances surrounding the…uh…wedding. I'm sure we can just explain—"

She gasped. "Any moment, they're going to find out that we're married and then all hell will break loose."

It was as if she hadn't even heard him.

"Kylie, I'm sure Cooper and Maxine aren't going to make a big deal out of our wedding. When we tell them what happened, they'll probably just laugh it off."

"I'm not talking about our *friends* finding out. I'm talking about my *family* finding out. My parents are here."

"Wait. Why are your parents here?"

"Because they've known Maxine practically as long as

I have. When we cheered at Boise State together, she used to come home with me for holidays and breaks. What am I supposed to tell my mom and dad?"

Funny, this was one complication he hadn't anticipated. "Well, let's go talk to your folks and let them know what happened and that we're trying to fix—"

"There you are, Kylie!" A very loud and very large man entered the ballroom with a smaller woman trailing behind him. "What's this I'm hearing about you being married?"

Drew took in the full beard and graying red hair of the older guy and decided this was one angry papa he did not want aiming a shotgun in his direction. But he had been raised right after all, so he stood up to meet the upcoming onslaught head-on.

"Dad, this is Drew." Kylie stood up as well and grabbed his arm, pressing her body against his side and pasting a huge grin on her face. "I've been dying for you to meet him."

More like dying of shame, but Drew wasn't going to contradict her. He swallowed his shock, happy that at least she was no longer wallowing in a puddle of despair. In fact, she seemed to be putting on quite the show of happy newlywed, gushing with happiness and squeezing his biceps.

"Hello, sir. I'm Lieutenant Commander Andrew Gregson. I'm glad we got the chance to meet before the reception started." Drew stuck out his hand, hoping Kylie's dad would take the hint that other guests were now filing into the ballroom and would bear witness to any potential scenes.

"Is Captain Cracker Jack here really your husband?" Mr. Chatterson was a behemoth of a man and all kinds of fired up as he eyeballed his new son-in-law. Drew couldn't blame the man for his anger, or his confusion, but Drew's forearm would soon get sore from holding it outstretched for so long.

"Dad, please," Kylie said when it became apparent that her father wasn't going to accept Drew's handshake. "People are looking. Don't make this any more awkward than it already is."

"Oh, Jellybean, you don't even know the definition of awkward. Try finding out from some tipsy busybody that my only daughter—my precious baby girl—robbed my dear, sweet wife of the opportunity to see her walk down the aisle."

Drew lowered his hand, because obviously Mr. Chatterson wasn't quite ready for social niceties.

"Dad, I'm sorry about that. Mom, I promise I'll make it up to you."

Drew fought the urge to not do a double take at Kylie's words. How could she make it up to her parents?

"It's actually a pretty funny story," Kylie continued. "We got married on a whim because the thought of waiting for a long engagement just seemed as if it would take forever, and we're just so crazy in love that we couldn't stand not to make it official."

"How long have you two known each other?" The man was right to look skeptical. Kylie was a horrible liar, but maybe that was just because Drew knew the truth. He decided to jump in and help her out.

"Not that long, sir, but it was love at first sight." His statement might not be any more honest than hers, but they must have felt *something* at first sight back in Reno. Why else would they have done such a crazy and reckless thing? To prove his claim, either to her parents or to himself, he leaned toward Kylie and placed a light kiss on her cheek.

She smelled like the gardenias in her forgotten bouquet, and it was all Drew could do not to pull her closer. Yet despite the intimate gesture, her face remained frozen, her fake smile firmly in place. But the pink color stealing up her chest and neck gave her away.

She'd felt it, too.

Unfortunately, they weren't alone, where they could explore this possible attraction further. In fact, they were knee-deep in the most undesirable conversation ever.

Mr. Chatterson did not look even slightly appeased. At least they were of the same height, so even if Drew couldn't pacify the man with his words, he wouldn't cower from his sheer size.

"Dad, you're overreacting," Kylie said, and it dawned on him that the dramatic apple didn't fall too far from the tree.

"Bobby." The smaller woman spoke up and nudged her husband's arm, nodding toward her new son-in-law. The older man finally reached out. Drew met his crushing grip, which gave no indication of Mr. Chatterson's willingness to back down. His wife intervened again by physically separating the men's fingers.

"Well, Andrew, I'm Kylie's mom, Lacey Chatterson." Mrs. Chatterson, dressed in an expensive and conservative pantsuit, was apparently the voice of reason in this family. "Why don't we all find our seats and get to know each other better?"

Kylie's father's shoulders deflated a bit. He must have realized his wife wasn't really asking a question or even making a suggestion. She was issuing an order.

"As much as Drew and I would love that," Kylie said, "we're seated up at the head table. Maybe after dinner we can come over and talk to you guys and explain our whirlwind romance. It's really quite a humorous story."

"Well, I'm not laughing," her dad said, his eyes not leaving Drew's face, as if sizing him up for future reference. "And you'd better figure out a date during the baseball off-season that we can set for the proper wedding."

What proper wedding?

The sound of glasses clinking saved them from any further appraisal. Kylie grabbed Drew's arm to pull him toward the dance floor, where the DJ was introducing the bride and groom and the rest of the wedding party. This was the second time she'd pulled him away from an uncomfortable situation tonight, and he was actually starting to get used to her long fingers touching him.

"It looks as if word spread pretty quickly," he whispered to her as they lined up near Mia and Alex Russell, one of the groomsmen.

If Drew thought Mr. Chatterson's looks could kill, it was nothing compared to the stink eye Kylie's friend Mia was directing his way. He'd seen suicide bombers looking friendlier right before launching themselves at Marine ground forces.

And there stood Cooper, his eyes lit up and his fist planted firmly over his smirking mouth. Drew knew their friends all had a million questions, and he wished to God he could have been the one to explain things to everyone. But heck, he couldn't even explain the situation to himself.

Kylie was standing tall, but her skin was flushed so pink, he could barely make out the few scattered freckles along her shoulders.

"I'm sorry," she whispered back. "I didn't mean for anyone to find out, especially not my family. I panicked when I saw my parents and didn't want them thinking I messed up. I know I kind of went overboard with the whole crazy-in-love bit back there, but there's no way Mia and Maxine will buy it, so we'll have to come clean with them, for the most part. Just don't tell anyone we were drunk when it happened. If we can ride this out for tonight, I'm sure we can come up with a good story so that nobody is the wiser when we announce later on that we're divorcing."

Divorce? He hated the sound of that word. He didn't know why. Logically, he knew it wasn't the worst thing that could happen to him, yet he didn't like the idea that he'd made a mistake. A reckless and impulsive mistake.

Unfortunately, there was no getting around it as they clearly couldn't stay married.

But at least he could move back to Boise at the end of summer when Luke returned from deployment. Kylie's life was here in Sugar Falls, and he didn't want her disgraced while he was in town. He wasn't going to have to live or work among these people or otherwise deal with the fall-out from their divorce. Or, hopefully, their annulment. So as much as it went against every controlling instinct in his body, he'd sit back and let her drive this crazy train in the way she saw fit. For now, at least.

When the DJ finished the introductions, they took their seats at the head table. The second Cooper and Maxine fixed themselves into their adjacent chairs, the bride leaned toward them and simply said, "Spill it."

And to Drew's shock, Kylie did just that. She told the small wedding party—including Mia and Alex, who came to stand behind them to hear the story better—about the night in Reno and how they'd gotten carried away and woken up with the marriage license and no memory of the night's events. Hadn't she *just* asked him not to tell anyone they'd been drinking?

Thankfully, she left out the more intimate details of how they awoke and how he'd barely been able to keep his hands or his eyes off her the following morning. Seeing her body in the clinging bridesmaid dress, he still was having a hard time not physically responding to her.

"So what are you going to do?" Mia asked, continuing

to stare at Drew as if he were an undercover spy sneaking into enemy territory.

"Well, originally we thought we'd just keep it a secret. But now we kind of pretended to everyone else that we were in love. It might've saved my reputation for the time being, but eventually we'll have to address it head-on and make it go away."

"Like get an annulment?" Maxine asked, and Kylie's telltale blush crept even farther up her cheeks.

"Or a divorce or something. We'd have to figure out what our legal options will be."

Again, the D-word hit him like a punch to the gut. Drew was trying to keep his opinions to himself, just like he usually kept his private life to himself. After all, since Kylie would be the one dealing with the social aftermath of their situation, he should probably let her take the lead on explaining things to everyone.

"I'm a dance teacher, not a lawyer," Mia started. "But I'm pretty sure you can get an annulment as long as you didn't consummate... Oh, no."

The look on Kylie's face must have given them away, because the ladies looked at their friend in shock, and Alex made a beeline straight toward the bar. But Cooper sat back in his chair and laughed until tears ran from his eyes.

"Oh, this is too good." Cooper's shoulders shook as he said the words. "Kylie and Saint Drew are married."

"You call him that, too?" Kylie asked.

"Everyone back on the base called him that. The guy doesn't get flustered. Ever. He's too calm and respectable for that. Gregson has a heart of gold, the tolerance of a martyr and the lifestyle of a monk."

"Really," Drew finally spoke up. "At a time like this, you two feel the need to compare descriptions of me?"

"No offense," Kylie said. "It's just that you're so perfect

and so nice to everyone. Even to that horrible Marcia and Elaine. Maybe if you hadn't forced me to stand there and make polite conversation with them, we wouldn't have let the cat out of the bag in the first place."

"Are you seriously blaming me for the fact that you were two seconds away from completely losing your temper and I was trying to be supportive?" The throbbing in Drew's neck was picking up speed, and he suddenly wondered if this lodge had a meditation room—or, at this point, a boxing speed bag—so he could go decompress and relieve some tension.

"How do you know I was about to lose anything? You don't even know me!"

"Uh-oh," Cooper said in a singsong voice, but not before her words hit their mark. "The newlyweds are having their first tiff."

Maxine made a shushing sound and pushed her husband's tuxedo-clad arm. The chief of police almost fell out of his chair, which would have made Drew smile if he didn't already feel as if he was three seconds away from punching his best friend himself.

"Uncle Drew!" The twins picked that moment to run over from the designated kids' table behind them. "Is it true that you married the tall lady that Aiden hit in the face?"

"*I* didn't hit her." Aiden shoved his brother. "*You* hit her. You always try to blame me for everything."

"Boys." Drew turned in his seat to break up the potential skirmish. "I thought we agreed that both of you were to blame for that incident."

He hated rehashing last night's video-game drama, but it was better than having to answer the eight-year-olds' questions about his unanticipated marriage and what it could potentially mean for them all. This past week, he'd found out that his nephews had a penchant for changing the subject on a dime and losing interest in an activity quicker than he could say "Reese's Peanut Butter Cup."

"But you *did* marry her, Uncle Drew?"

"Is she gonna be our aunt now?"

"Is she gonna come live with us at the cabin?"

"Will she bring more bubbles with her?"

The rapid-fire questions just went to show that the one time he actually wanted to divert the boys' attention, they decided to hold on tenaciously like a heat missile on target launch.

He looked at his wife, hoping she would have some answers, because he sure as heck didn't want to be blamed for saying the wrong thing.

"Hey, boys." Kylie motioned them over. "Did you see that they're going to have a chocolate fountain after they cut the cake?"

Alex Russell's father and grandfather came over to congratulate the bride and groom and temporarily distracted the rest of the wedding party. Meanwhile, Drew listened to his nephews' squeals as Kylie spoke with them about all the marshmallows and fruit and edibles that would be stacked by the fountain.

He couldn't believe the instant rapport Kylie had with the boys. Aiden and Caden were cheerfully animated as they talked to her. She listened attentively, nodding her head as if their opinion on the proper skewering order of treats was the most important discussion she would have this evening. For the first time in the past hour, he found himself grinning.

He'd probably been just as smitten with her that evening in Reno. At the time, he had blamed his reaction to her on everything from the amount of alcohol he'd drunk to the amount of time he'd gone without a date. And maybe now, with the boys being so starved for female attention that any caring woman was a novelty for them, he could argue that his tenderness toward her came from a sense of gratitude.

He was a man of science and normally didn't listen to gut instincts, but he couldn't shake the feeling that his re-action to her was caused by none of those things. It was just Kylie.

There was definitely something about her that attracted people. And there was also something about her that had his normally out-of-control nephews thinking she was next best thing to chocolate-covered marshmallows.

He couldn't help but appreciate her sweet and nurturing way with the boys. Heaven knew the twins could benefit from having someone like Kylie in their lives. And to be honest, Drew could use the help supervising them.

"Seriously, though, I gotta ask." Cooper, having fin-ished talking to the Russell men, leaned in and spoke quietly. "Kylie and Saint Drew? How did you manage to make that happen?"

"I have no idea," Drew answered honestly.

"Well, how are you going to fix it?"

Kylie stood to walk the kids back to the designated chil-dren's table, and he heard her explaining how the servers were going to be bringing them chicken strips. She told them if they promised to wash their hands afterward and wait until all the other guests got a turn at the fountain, they'd be able to dip treats to their hearts' content.

Drew shook his head.

"I have no idea," he repeated.

He watched her retreating backside clad in the form-fitting satin dress and thought he could get used to watch-ing her successfully manage his nephews. Heck, he could get used to simply watching her...

* * *

Kylie had avoided the dance floor and her parents for most of the reception. But she knew her stay of execution was temporary. She planted herself in her seat throughout dinner, the champagne toast and the cake-cutting ceremony, biding her time and trying to figure out how to deal with this stupid situation she'd gotten herself into. It was one thing to get married to a stranger, quite another to pretend she was madly in love with him.

Damn. She'd really bitten off more than she could chew this time. But she wouldn't dare allow her mom and dad to think that she didn't know what she was doing or that she couldn't handle this on her own.

When she was growing up, her parents had always told her that she let her impulsivity and her independence get the best of her. As the baby, with four protective older brothers, the family joke was that Kylie was quick to make a decision, and quicker to do things by herself, refusing to let anyone of them help her. Ever. When she was three years old, they were on a winter holiday and Kevin tried to lace up her snow boots so they could go outside sledding. She told him she could do it herself and she did. The problem was, by the time she'd finally gotten them knotted on tight enough, it was already dark and her brothers were coming inside for dinner.

She'd brought this mess on herself and, as they said in the pageant world, sometimes the best way to deal with an uncomfortable situation was to fake it until you made it.

"We have a special request for the newlyweds." The DJ made the announcement as the bars to a new song came out through the speakers. Kylie looked at the bride and groom, who had been talking to some guests across the room but were now looking at straight at her. "But not the chief and Mrs. Cooper," the DJ said into his microphone.

When the guests began to mumble to each other, she realized why everyone was turning in her direction. Oh, no. It couldn't be. Who would've requested this song? She prayed the guy wasn't going to say what she thought he was going to say.

But when the opening notes to the love ballad came on, she knew.

"So please welcome Dr. and Mrs. Gregson to the dance floor to celebrate their recent marriage." She had no idea where her new husband was or even if he wanted to be found. He must have thought she was completely nuts for wanting to pretend their marriage was real.

All the guests were looking at her and probably assuming the exact same thing: *Kylie Chatterson can't even get her own husband to dance with her.* She thought about ducking into the ladies' room, but how could she when all eyes were on her? By the time Michael Bolton began the opening lines of the song, Kylie couldn't take the stares anymore. She was about to turn and run when she felt that velvetlike steel hand on her for the second time that day.

"I guess we better give the crowd what they want," Drew said as he tugged on her elbow, forcing her to stand, and then escorted her toward the dance floor. She looked down at his hand and saw that his gold wedding band was now on his finger. Where had that come from? She could've sworn she hadn't seen it earlier, during the ceremony.

"Did you set this up?" She didn't mean to sound accusatory, but her friends wouldn't have pulled a stunt like this.

"Me?" he asked. "God, no. I hate to dance. I'm terrible at it."

And when he took her into his strong arms, she realized he wasn't lying. Drew really was a terrible dancer. The best he could manage was a reenactment of an awk-

ward junior high slow-dance version of locked arms and
feet shuffling side to side. After he'd stepped on her toes
for the third time, she finally pulled him in closer to her,
wrapping her arms around his neck. "Here, just hold me
close and sway to the beat."

She'd been a cheerleader in high school and college
and adored dancing. How could she have married someone with two left feet? Wouldn't she have at least danced
with him that night in Reno before they'd had too much to
drink and headed off to the Silver Rush Wedding Chapel?

The wool of his dress uniform was coarse under her
fingers, and she was tempted to move her hands toward
the tan smoothness of the back of his neck. To touch the
soft skin she remembered feeling in that hotel bed.

Side to side. She needed to keep swaying, to keep moving, before she did something stupid.

She'd danced with plenty of guys before, but never one
who matched her so well in size. Or who smelled so great.
Her nose was centimeters away from his upper jaw, and
she inhaled his scent of lemongrass and fresh pine. His
arms were like steel bands around her waist, and if she
closed her eyes, she could almost pretend she and Drew
were alone.

Almost.

She made the mistake of glancing around the room before looking back at Drew's face.

Kylie moved her body closer to his so he wouldn't be
able to penetrate her with that all-knowing blue gaze like
a microscope looking deep into her.

She could feel his pulse beating against the neckline of
her dress, and warmth spread through her. Maybe she'd
been too hasty, because his stare might've been the lesser
of two evils.

"I was just wondering who could've set up this little

song request." She was having difficulty drawing an even breath; her voice came out as barely a whisper.

"I have no idea," he answered, his cheek pressing against her temple as he spoke into her ear. "Besides the wedding party, I don't really know many of the guests."

"I thought your family had a cabin here. Didn't you grow up in Sugar Falls?"

"No. I'm from Boise originally. But we spent a lot of summers up here when I was a kid."

"Ah, so you're one of the bankrollers," Kylie said, referring to the wealthy tourists who provided a brisk business for many of the locals.

"Hardly. Before they retired, my dad was a minister and my mom was a teacher. Her grandparents owned the cabin, and she inherited it when they passed. So we definitely aren't part of the elite visiting class."

"Oh, wow. That really explains a lot."

"What's that supposed to mean?" She heard the offended tone in his question and cursed herself. She hadn't meant to insult his family's financial status.

"I meant about you having a preacher for a father. It must be why you're such a Goody Two-shoes." Ugh, that probably didn't sound like any less of an insult.

"Trust me. My father's profession was no guarantee for the way I turned out."

At that point, Kylie did lean back to look at his eyes. "I find that hard to believe."

"Okay, so I really wasn't all that bad. But my twin brother, Luke, was the proverbial preacher's kid. He was always in trouble. Kind of like my nephews over there." He looked toward the chocolate fountain and the kids, who were using the treat-covered skewers to do their best impression of bloodthirsty pirates. "So you'd think I'd know how to handle them better. I should probably get over there before they stab someone's eye out."

"Nah, they have marshmallows blunting the ends of their swords. The worst damage they could do is knock the fountain over. Right onto Elaine and Marcia, if we're lucky."

Drew's lips angled upward before he recovered his perfect countenance. But the small glimpse of him letting down his guard showed her he did have a sense of humor.

The song drew to a close and the booming beats for the next one started up. Several shrieking women ran toward the parquet floor. Normally, Kylie would've loved to stay put and shake her stuff with the other dancers. But after witnessing Drew's lack of rhythm to a slow song, she didn't want to be an accomplice to what he might be capable of with a fast tempo.

"Your dad is staring this way. I think he's trying to get your attention," Drew said.

She loved and respected her parents, and they deserved the truth. But not tonight. She would see them tomorrow before they left for Seattle and explain things to them then—without Drew there. Kylie saw her mother talking to the manager of the Snow Creek Lodge, her smile bright and her hands gesturing wildly toward centerpieces and the outside terrace.

Uh-oh. She knew that determined look on her mother's happy face. How had she let things get this far? Lacey Chatterson obviously had it in her head that Kylie and Drew were actually willing to go through with their wedding again, just so the mother of the bride could plan a dream reception for her daughter.

A daughter who had run off and married a stranger in secret, then stood there in front of her adoring parents and pretended to be madly in love. She gave a little finger wave toward her dad as her insides twisted up in guilt.

"Maybe we should grab something to drink and make our way over there," Drew said, reminding her they were just standing there in the center of the room.

"Oh, they're fine. I can see them tomorrow and clear everything up then."

His palm remained on the small of her back as he leaned toward her ear so she could hear him over the loud lyrics of the Commodores. "You don't have to face your parents, or the rest of the town, alone. Remember when I said we'd be in this together? I really meant it."

She'd thought he'd meant they'd be in it together only if there was a baby involved. So why was he sticking around now that he'd been cleared of official daddy status? She wouldn't blame him if he made a run for the nearest creek. But he remained right beside her, a blue-uniformed wall of muscle that, judging by the sincere look in his eyes, left no doubt that he wasn't going anywhere. For tonight, at least.

"Of course," he said as he guided her off the dance floor and toward the open bar set up in the corner, "if having me there would just make things more awkward or embarrassing for you, say the word."

She jerked her head so that she could face him. What was he saying? Would he want to explain their marriage to *his* parents without *her* there? She looked down at her cleavage and decided that with a minister for a father, he probably would. She tried not to feel insulted, but what did she expect? He was Saint Drew. And she was...

Well, she was Kylie Chatterson. She was known to be a little brassy at times and not too conservative in her fashion choices, which usually showed off her curves to great advantage. Although she was smart and successful and came from a loving family, she probably wasn't Drew's first choice of a woman to take home to meet the folks.

And if it weren't for her impulsiveness and hot temper, he probably wouldn't have had to meet hers, either. Even though neither of them knew who was to blame for their predicament in the first place, she was definitely the only one who could mitigate the current awkwardness.

"Listen, that's very thoughtful of you to offer to come with me to talk to them. I know my dad can be a lot to take, and he isn't in the warmest of moods right this second. Why don't we just drop it for tonight and try to act as normal as possible?"

"Define *normal*. Because frankly, I'm having a hard time keeping up with what's normal nowadays," he said as they approached the bar.

Was he talking about her love-at-first-sight pretense?

"Sorry for the whole lovey-dovey routine earlier. I truly don't make a habit out of lying to anyone, least of all my parents. But I was trying to avoid a big I-told-you-so moment. My dad is always telling me that I'm too impulsive. I guess I just wanted to prove that I had a good reason for what we did and that I had everything under control. I'm sure you thought I was off my rocker for implying that the marriage was anything more than a drunken mistake."

Drew cringed at her statement. What had she said wrong?

"So just so that we're on the same page," he said carefully, "you want me to go along with this charade until tomorrow, when you start announcing to the world that I was a big mistake?"

Ooh. *That* was why he had cringed. "No, *you're* not the mistake. Getting drunk and getting married was the mistake. Come on, you couldn't possibly think that any woman in her right mind wouldn't jump at the chance to be married to someone as perfect as you?"

Clearly, she was *not* in her right mind. As soon as she saw his lips curve upward, another rush of heat stole up her skin. Why in the world had she just said that out loud? She must be as red as the jar of maraschino cherries at the bar.

"A champagne for the lady, and I'll take a Coke," he said to the bartender, his warm fingers still splayed against her back. Apparently he wasn't taking any chances on drinking alcohol in her presence again. He probably figured that someone needed to be sober to make sure she didn't do or say anything else outlandish tonight.

It was just as well. The twins ran up to them as Drew handed her a crystal flute. "Uncle Drew, Aunt...uh... what's her name?" Caden stage-whispered to his brother, whose face was smeared with chocolate from ear to ear.

"It's Kyle," Aiden whispered back.

"Are we s'pose to call her Aunt Kyle?" Caden asked.

"How about you just call me Kylie?" she said, correcting their pronunciation by putting emphasis on the *e* sound at the end of her name. The boys really were too cute for words. She suspected Drew and his own brother had been just as spunky and just as mischievous as these two when they were kids.

"But Kyle is a boy's name," Caden said. "And you're not a boy."

"Kylieeeee," she repeated, then pointed at her dad. "You can talk to that big redheaded man over there at that table. He's the one who gave me such a confusing name."

The twins looked at her father, a lumberjack of a man who, at one time or another, had intimidated some of the best batters in professional baseball.

"Nah, that's okay." Aiden shook his head. "Anyway,

they're building a bonfire outside and me and Caden wanted to go out with the other kids and watch."

Drew looked at her, lifting his shoulders up as if to ask her opinion. The man gave off the most capable and competent vibe 90 percent of the time, but he really was lost when it came to his nephews.

She didn't know the boys well enough to trust them around fire without adult supervision. But then she saw Scooter and Jonesy, a couple of retired volunteer firefighters, leading a line of kids outside like the Pied Pipers of Sugar Falls, and told Drew she thought it would be a safe enough activity.

The kids scampered off, and she and her new husband wove their way through chairs and tables until they reached the empty head table—where her parents made a beeline for them.

"So let's cut to the chase," Bobby Chatterson said before pulling out the chairs reserved for the bride and groom. "Did you knock my daughter up, or what?"

"Dad," Kylie pleaded, although it wasn't until this morning that she'd been able to rule that possibility out.

"No, sir." Drew didn't bat an eye. "It really happened quite suddenly. And please believe me when I say that I would never have eloped with Kylie if I'd thought it would cause her any problems with her family."

That was mostly true. Her husband was likely well trained in phrasing things just the right way in order to calm people down. Of course, what he'd left unsaid was that he probably would never have married Kylie ever. Period.

"That's good to know," her dad said. "Because Kylie not having a proper wedding would really be a big disappointment to her mom and me. So I put a call into my buddy who runs the stadium club back home. He owes me a pretty big favor and thinks he can get your reception on the books for October."

Oh, no.

Drew, who had been taking a healthy chug of his soda, choked a bit.

Kylie sighed. "Dad, seriously. We're not going to have a wedding reception back in Seattle."

"Fine, then." Her father threw his hands up in the air. "Have it here. Your mom already spoke to the manager, and he'll give us a pretty good rate if we put down the deposit tomorrow."

Thankfully she was sitting beside Drew, because she couldn't even imagine seeing the mortified look crossing his face right that second. "Slow down, Dad. There's no need to rush into any of this."

"You're really not one to preach about rushing into anything, Jellybean."

"I have a suggestion." Drew's voice was calm and his fingers were soothing as he lightly stroked her bare shoulders. When had he put his arm around her? "Why don't we all sleep on it tonight, and then we can get together tomorrow and throw some ideas around for the big reception. Maybe come up with a game plan that everyone will be happy with."

Kylie took a drink of champagne to keep her jaw from dropping. What was he thinking?

"I like a good game plan," her dad said. "You good with that, Lace?"

Her mom stood up. "I'm good with anything that gets your mouth to stop jabbering and your feet to start moving. Get your dancing shoes on, Bobby. It's time to show these kids how to shake it."

"All right, we'll see you two tomorrow, then," her father said. "Wait, we're gonna need directions to your place."

"You don't remember how to get to my condo?" Kylie asked at the exact same time Drew responded, "The cabin's a little ways out of town, off Sweetwater Bend."

Her husband was looking at something outside on the terrace and must not have been paying attention when he'd made the slip.

"What cabin?" Her mom lifted a brown eyebrow. Her parents had seized on the discrepancy immediately. How was she going to extricate herself from this one?

"Well, it's only been a week, so we're still sorting out the...uh...living arrangements," she said.

"Hmm." Her father stroked his well-groomed beard. "It's probably better you don't live together just yet anyway. I can't really see you sharing your shoe closet with a couple of little boys. Plus, there's no way could you rough it out in some cabin in the woods."

"What do you mean, Dad? I could live in a cabin anywhere." The trapped feeling she'd been experiencing just seconds ago was now building up into defensiveness. She felt like a grenade—and her father was about to pull the pin.

"Sure you could." Her dad winked at her mom, and Kylie exploded.

"Dad, I'm thirty years old. I can live wherever I want and with whomever I want. And if I decide to move in with *my* husband and *our* nephews into *our* cabin, then that's what I'll do, because I'm an adult, and I can make my own decisions."

"Fine. I'm sure you know what's best, Jellybean. By the way, your brother Kane is still recovering from his shoulder surgery and has been eager to get out of Chicago and recuperate somewhere in private. I'll let him know he can stay at your condo since you won't be using it."

"Perfect. That settles everything," Lacey Chatterson

said, pulling her husband toward the dance floor. "We'll see you two lovebirds tomorrow at the cabin."

Ugh! She'd just done it again. Kylie'd let her temper get the best of her, and now she couldn't backpedal without making her parents suspect something was up.

And as if the hole she'd dug for herself couldn't get any bigger, Drew wouldn't—or couldn't—even look at her.

Chapter Five

Drew would've tried to stop the words before they came out of Kylie's mouth if he hadn't been staring so intently at the raging fire looming bigger and closer outside. Where were the twins—and why weren't the smoke alarms going off?

While he couldn't very well have a stranger move in with him and the boys, especially one who didn't know how to keep her hotheaded responses in check, dealing with that issue wasn't topping his list of priorities at that exact moment. He needed to get out there and make sure his nephews weren't in danger of setting the Snow Creek Lodge ablaze.

More guests were trickling outside to enjoy the brisk evening air along with the robust flames in the circular stone pit. Drew was relieved to see the fire did in fact look well contained, but he couldn't say the same about his nephews.

They were nowhere to be seen.

"What's wrong?" Kylie asked as she walked up behind him. He didn't know if she'd followed him so she could explain her outburst about moving into the cabin with him, or if she could instinctively tell that he was worried about something.

But either way, he was glad she was by his side.

"I don't see the boys." He looked back and forth, taking in every person in the dim firelight. But none of them were identical four-foot troublemakers with impish faces and springy blond curls.

"Okay. Let's think about this logically." Sure, *now* Miss Hothead could be logical. Where was her rational thinking just a few moments ago?

"It's only been fifteen minutes since they came out here," she continued. "About five minutes ago, I looked out the glass doors and saw them helping the bigger boys bring more wood over. So they couldn't have gotten far in that amount of time."

He appreciated her awareness of the twins while he'd been focused on calming her father down, but she apparently didn't realize just exactly *what* kind of chaos Caden and Aiden were capable of wreaking in that short amount of time.

He started yelling their names, but Kylie grabbed his hand and squeezed it tightly. "Let's not start a full-fledged panic. You go toward the ski lift and search for them there. I'll ask if anyone has seen them."

Drew nodded before running toward the motorized benches that hauled adventure enthusiasts up to the top of the mountain. He was really going to let the boys have it if he found them messing around on the lifts after he'd expressly told them not to get close to that area.

But the chairs were motionless, suspended in the dark

night air, and the control room with the engine and levers was tightly locked.

Where could they be?

He tried not to let the worst-case scenario sink in, but concern was wedging itself firmly in his throat. He'd promised his brother he'd look after them. What if he'd lost them out here in the forest? At least it was no longer snow season. But still, it was dark and the area was pretty remote. They could've wandered too far and gotten lost, or worse—separated.

He wondered if they were scared. One time, when he'd been five years old, he'd spotted a giant gumball machine in the Boise mall. He'd been so in awe, he'd slipped away from his mom and Luke to check it out, and before he knew it, they were nowhere to be seen. He remembered his dad had always told him that if he ever got lost, he should stay in the same place, and that was just what Drew had done. Of course, the place he'd decided to stay was wedged behind a table and a trash can in the busy food court. So nobody had been able to find him for nearly thirty minutes. It had been the scariest and longest half hour of his life. He'd cried so hard and so silently, he'd nearly made himself sick.

Two high school girls had found him and took him to their gift-wrap booth, where they were volunteering to wrap presents for their cheerleading squad's fund-raiser. One girl had held his hand while the other had flagged down a security guard to report a lost boy.

Drew's mom was there in minutes and looked just as panicked as he had felt. But worse was seeing his twin brother, Luke, who had been more upset than all of them and had also gotten sick in fear for his lost sibling. Drew tried to play off the experience as if he hadn't been frightened out of his mind and promised himself that it was better to be calm and organized in a crisis than to lose control of his emotions.

Yet here he was thirty years later, experiencing that lost, scared and helpless sensation all over again. He needed to find the boys. He needed to take control of the situation so he wouldn't feel so overwhelmed.

He ran back toward the terrace, deciding that he would enlist an entire search party if need be, but he was going to do *something*. Yet right before he got to the terrace, he caught sight of a tall redhead walking through a darkened field of overgrown grass just beyond the north end of the lodge. He probably wouldn't have seen her if it hadn't been for the way the distant glow of the fire caught the glimmering sparkle of her gold-colored bridesmaid dress.

Drew jogged past the patio and straight for her. As he got closer, he saw that she was holding the hands of two animated blond-haired eight-year-olds. One of the boys was dragging a broken tree limb behind them.

"Where were you two?" His voice cracked, the fear and anguish he'd just experienced overriding any sense of relief or gratitude for Kylie having found them.

"We were just getting more wood for the bonfire," said Aiden, or possibly Caden. It was too dark and Drew's adrenaline was pumping too fast for him to discern the difference.

"Yeah, Mr. Scooter and Mr. Jonesy said they couldn't make the fire too big without more tinder, so we went to find them some. Why are you all sweaty and breathing funny like that, Uncle Drew?"

Kylie bent down and spoke softly, calmly. "Your uncle was worried because he couldn't find you."

"But we told Hunter where we were going."

"That's who told me where to find them," Kylie said to Drew. "We already talked about it, and they both promised me that next time they decided to go off exploring, they'd tell an adult."

"Hunter's eleven. He's almost a grown-up," Caden argued.

"But Hunter's not responsible for you two. I am." He was at his wit's end, but he knew yelling at the boys wouldn't solve anything.

"Sorry, Uncle Drew. We were just trying to help make the fire grow bigger."

He let out the breath he hadn't realized he'd been holding. He'd been deployed to the front lines of enemy territory all over the world. He was trained to maintain his cool, to help other people get through their emotional issues. But this? It was too much. He'd been back in the United States for a little over a week and already he'd gotten rip-roaring drunk, married a stranger, pissed off his in-laws and practically lost his brother's children. War was easier.

His mom had been wrong. He couldn't handle the boys. He couldn't handle any of this. And he had to report to his new job assignment the day after tomorrow. How was he supposed to counsel wounded veterans and PTSD patients when he couldn't even control his own life?

His sister was volunteering at some orphanage in West Africa, his brother was on a top secret assignment and his parents were on a much-needed vacation. He had no one. For the second time in his life, Drew felt completely and utterly alone.

Where were the cheerleaders at the mall gift-wrap booth when he needed them most?

"Okay, boys." Kylie's voice broke the direction of his self-pitying thoughts. "Why don't you haul that branch over to the fire pit? But do not step off that concrete patio without talking to your uncle first."

As the boys made their way back, Kylie and Drew stayed near the stone wall separating the lodge from the overgrown trails beyond. She stood close to him as he got his breathing under control.

Her skin glowed golden in the firelight, and he knew she must be freezing cold. Even though it was June, the nights up here in the mountains still dipped into the fifties, and she was barely covered in that tight satin sheath. In fact, her shoulders shivered slightly. He took his wool uniform jacket off and put it over her shoulders. The woman might lose her temper with the gossips of Sugar Falls and her overbearing father, but she sure knew how to keep her cool around his nephews.

"Thank you," she said as she snuggled into the jacket's warmth. They were both keeping an eye on the boys, yet neither one was in too much of a hurry to gather around the fire or otherwise return to the wedding reception.

"No, I should be thanking *you*. I ran off hell-bent for leather, and you kept your wits about you and found the boys single-handedly."

"Did you just say *hell*, Saint Drew?" She looked up into his eyes, and when he saw the faint smile on her full lips, he was tempted to show her exactly how unsaintly he could be.

"Contrary to what everyone thinks about me, I'm no angel." Especially not with the way his overheated body was responding to her closeness.

She tilted her head as if considering such an absurd possibility. But then something caught her eye, and he followed her gaze to where her parents were standing just inside the ballroom, saying their goodbyes to the bride and groom.

She sighed. "I'm sorry about inviting myself to live in

your cabin with you and the boys. I promise that I never had any intention of putting you in that situation."

"So you're not really considering moving in with me?"

"As if." She tried to laugh, but the sound came out more strangled than anything else. "Can you imagine how awkward that would be?"

He didn't answer because, although he knew that it would be uncomfortable for them in some ways, it would also be a perfect solution to his biggest problem. "I don't think it would be so bad."

"Are you kidding? We barely know each other, and you've already got your hands full with the boys and your new job and everything."

"But where will you go? I mean, you could back down in front of your parents, but they did sort of call your bluff by saying your brother would be staying at your place."

"Ugh. I forgot about that. And Kane tells my dad everything. I guess I could move in with Mia or get a room here at the Lodge."

"For the entire summer?"

"Why do you sound as if you don't think the idea of me staying at your cabin is completely ridiculous?"

Was he that obvious?

"Well, sure, it might seem odd at first. But technically, we *are* married. I mean, nobody else in town would think it was unusual. And to be honest with you, I could use some help with the boys."

"But I don't know anything about kids."

"You've done a better job in the past twenty-four hours than I've done all week. Maybe it's because you're a woman and they need a mother figure, but you have a way with them. They actually listen to you and follow your directions. Look, just stay for a little while until I can learn how to do it on my own. Remember what I've been saying since the start? We're in this together."

"You know, you're way better at this whole psychology thing than I am."

"Years of training."

"Speaking of years of training, I have a full-time job. I guess I could do some work from home, but I couldn't be with the boys all the time." She was caving. He could sense it from the way she seemed to be examining it from all the angles.

"I have them enrolled in a summer day camp, but I would still need help with drop-offs and pickups and putting out any other fires—no pun intended—that might come up."

Just then, her parents walked outside. As Kylie moved in closer to him and looped her arm through his, Drew knew her dad's still suspicious expression sealed the deal for her. He was about to get a new roommate.

"Well, Jellybean, your mom and I are heading to our room upstairs for the night. We'll stop by for dinner on our way out of town tomorrow. Should we bring anything?"

"Nope," Drew said. He wasn't going to let her back out now. "We'll have everything all taken care of."

He should be wondering how he'd come up with this mad scheme, let alone gotten Kylie to agree to it. But all he could think about was how soft his new wife and roommate's skin was.

Kylie drove down the rutted dirt lane leading to the Gregson family cabin. Her Mercedes was stuffed to its closed convertible top with all the shoes, clothes and bedding that she might need for the next couple of months—or at least until her brother was no longer staying at her condo.

Of all the stupid scrapes she'd gotten herself into, putting on that newlywed act for her parents last night really took the cake. She couldn't believe she'd be stuck playing live-in nanny for some handsome stranger for the summer.

Her head was still throbbing from the two glasses of champagne she'd indulged in at the reception last night. When was she going to learn that alcohol and Andrew Gregson did not mix well for her?

She put the car in Park and eyeballed her temporary new home before getting out. The log house was small, but it seemed to be in good repair. Although the dirt driveway was going to be killer on her high heels.

She grabbed a suitcase out of the front of her two-seater coupe just as Drew came down the porch steps. "Here, let me help you with your… Hey, is all of this stuff yours?"

He squinted at the loaded trunk, and she saw his Adam's apple bob up, then down.

She had about two hours to settle in before her parents showed up for a home-cooked Sunday dinner and Act Two of her cozying up to her pretend husband.

She didn't have time to deal with Drew's analysis of her belongings. She handed him the suitcase and a tote bag stuffed with shoes before grabbing her purse, her laptop case and a paper sack full of groceries from Duncan's Market. Thankfully, Marcia Duncan hadn't been in the store when she had stopped to get supplies for tonight's meal.

Drew was dressed in jeans and a button-up plaid shirt that still had creases in it. Which only drew her gaze to his very large, very broad shoulders.

Ugh, she needed to stop looking at his body.

Instead, as they walked up to the path to the front porch, she focused on the old brown Oldsmobile sedan parked along the side of the house.

"Where's the Man Machine?" she asked.

"The what?" He looked over his shoulder at her.

"The big yellow Jeep. That's what Maxine used to call it when Cooper was staying here and driving that thing."

"It's parked near the boat shed out back. Why would she call it that?"

"Why wouldn't she? It has huge mud tires, a gun locker strapped to the rear bumper and a beer cooler as the center console. It's about as manly a vehicle as it gets."

"Hmm, well, the twins thought it was fun, but I decided my grandma's Oldsmobile would be a safer choice for a family car."

She hitched her purse higher on her shoulder as she leaned in to look inside the car more suitable for a great-grandmother than for a bachelor uncle. "It only has lap belts and no airbags. Plus six ashtrays and not a single cup holder. How kid friendly do you think that is?"

"Well, it's better than that little red matchbox you're screaming around town in."

"That's a Mercedes-Benz. It's my style—sophisticated with just a hint of pizzazz."

Were they having their first argument? If so, he needed to understand that just because he was an uptight doctor didn't mean she was going to give up her plush lifestyle to be some Suzie Homemaker wife and substitute mother.

He held the front door open for her, polite even in disagreement.

"She's here! Aunt Kylie's finally here," Caden screamed as he ran out into the living room in nothing but a pair of superhero costume leggings.

Okay, so maybe her heart melted just a tiny bit when she heard the word *aunt*. Although Hunter called her the same thing, her own brothers had yet to have any children—that she knew of—and she didn't mind the idea of these delightful cuties looking up to her.

Aiden followed, wearing only his underwear and the top half of the costume, complete with a cape around his shoulders. "Hey, Aunt Kylie, you wanna sleep in the bunk room with me and Aiden?"

"First, *you're* Aiden and that—" she pointed to the shirtless boy opening the kitchen cupboards "—is Caden. Don't try to pull that old trick on me. Second, let me get all my stuff unpacked before we figure out the sleeping arrangements."

She knew Drew wouldn't want to sleep in the same bed with her. Really, she had to agree it was for the best, no matter how good he looked when he woke up. But she really hoped she wasn't sleeping in the bunk room.

"I was thinking that I could room with the boys," Drew said as if responding to her exact thought. The guy was both moral *and* chivalrous. "There are two sets of bunk beds in there. You can take the master bedroom."

"Are you sure? How are you going to fit in a bunk bed?" Again her eyes strayed to his bulky shoulders and long, strong legs. She needed to stop looking at him if she was going to be living here. No good could come of lusting for her in-name-only husband.

"Trust me. Navy ships have much smaller and crowded quarters than these. We'll make do." He lowered his voice so the boys wouldn't hear. "Besides, I'll keep most of my stuff where it is and just sneak into one of the bunks after the kids fall asleep. I figure we should probably give off the appearance that we're sharing a room, even with the boys, so they don't slip and say something later."

"You're probably right," she said while simultaneously thinking, *How in the world are we going to fake this all summer?*

"Boys, come help get Miss, ah…" He lowered his voice again. "What do you want them to call you?"

Well, technically, she was no longer a miss. Was Drew going to expect her to take his last name while they were living here together, pretending to be the happily married couple? They had so much to figure out. What the kids called her seemed like the simplest of issues.

"Kylie is fine. Whatever they're comfortable with." Although she did like the aunt part, she didn't want to force her questionably earned title on Drew or his family.

He carried her suitcase toward the hallway. After dropping the bag of groceries on the kitchen table, she followed him for the rest of the tour.

The cabin was one large great room, consisting of an open floor plan kitchen, a comfortable living room and a dining room table separating the two. A hallway led toward what she assumed were the bedrooms and a single bathroom.

"Wow, you have a ton of books," she said when she saw the cardboard boxes lining the larger bedroom wall. "Are they all yours?"

"Yep. My mom and dad were cleaning out the garage and wanted me to take some of my stuff. I told them I'd go through the boxes over the summer and see what I can get rid of. When Luke gets back and I get a place of my own, it'll make the move easier."

Whew. It was a good reminder that Drew was in Sugar Falls for only a short time. Hopefully, come September, this whole awkward mess would be behind them.

He effortlessly tossed her oversize suitcase, which had to weigh close to seventy-five pounds, on top of the bright orange-and-turquoise-patterned quilt spread out on the bed. Realizing the strong man could probably lift her just as easily and place her on the king-size mattress, Kylie figured she needed all the reminding she could get that this arrangement was temporary.

She averted her face, which must have been an unflattering shade of crimson, and tried to concentrate on the contents of the boxes.

Psychology textbooks, philosophy books, books on world religions. He was an intellectual man.

And a seriously good-looking one.

"So I better finish unloading my car. My parents will be here in a couple of hours, and I wanted to make some dinner and at least make a pretense of being all settled in." Plus, she had a half-gallon container of Neapolitan ice cream melting in her grocery sack.

"Are they coming armed with bridal magazines?"

"I hope not. I told them that you didn't want to talk about reception plans with your nephews here because you didn't want them thinking that our marriage wasn't legitimate. So with any luck, we'll just have dinner and they'll hit the road."

"You have no idea how good a home-cooked meal sounds. The boys and I have been living off peanut-butter-and-jelly sandwiches and frozen chicken nuggets."

She looked at his flat stomach and wondered how much food it must take to keep his body looking so muscular and taut.

"I…uh…actually wasn't going to make a true home-cooked meal. I just picked up a roasted chicken from Duncan's and some stuff for a salad. I'm not really much of a chef, but I thought I could manage a box of rice pilaf. So don't get your hormones…I mean your taste buds too worked up."

Ugh. She sounded like an idiot. What kind of woman stood in man's bedroom and talked about hormones and getting worked up? He, like the rest of the town, probably thought she was beyond promiscuous, coming on to him like this.

He studied her from behind the metal-rimmed glasses, and she wished she could figure out what he was thinking whenever he looked at her. He stared at her as if she was some obscure test subject he could study and later write about in his own psychology textbook.

"Uncle Drew." An anxious voice interrupted the tension in the room. "Come quick! Aiden got his cape stuck in the post of the top bunk. And it won't come off his neck."

"Ah, jeez…" Drew said before running out of the room.

She would follow him to help. But she had to get her pulse and her mixed emotions in check before she could be of any use to anyone.

Unfortunately, her familiar litany of prime factors was short-lived. Drew yelled, "Kylie, could you come help us out?"

"What's wrong?" she asked as she entered the boys' room. But she knew the answer before Caden could control his laughter enough to tell her.

Drew was holding Aiden's suspended body, which was still clad only in the top half of the superhero costume and his underwear. But it wasn't Aiden's makeshift cape that was stuck in the bed rails. It was the little boy's curly blond head.

Bless her husband, who was trying to sound calm but looked about as frazzled as a pageant contestant who'd run out of double-sided tape. "His head is wedged in here pretty well, and I'm worried that if I let go of his body to help dislodge him, he might asphyxiate."

A good-looking and well-built man standing near her bed in a master bedroom, she could barely deal with. But this…well, *this* was a no-brainer for her. Kylie tried to keep her laughter in check as she said, "Hold him steady while I go grab something from the kitchen."

Chapter Six

An hour and two sticks of butter later, the twins were sitting on the rag rug in the living room, wearing headphones and playing a math game on Drew's tablet. Well, Drew hoped it was a math game. He'd set up parental controls the first day they got here, but these boys had proved to be tech-savvy enough to bypass those restrictions if they got an idea to. But at least they were behaving for once.

A loud knock sounded at the cabin's front door, and he said a silent prayer, hoping to get through tonight without scolding his nephews or insulting Kylie's parents. He sure hoped the Shadowview Military Hospital had a gym for employees, because Drew knew exactly where he would be spending his lunch hours this summer, working off steam.

Kylie's heels pinged along the hardwood floor as she rushed out of the kitchen and toward the door. As his wife ushered her parents into the cabin, for a second Drew wondered if they'd look down their noses at his humble family's little log house. Now that he'd seen Kylie's flashy red sports car and her mother's even flashier diamond ring, he guessed the Chatterson family was used to the finer things in life.

But the couple smiled brightly as Lacey handed over a bouquet of peonies to Kylie and Mr. Chatterson passed him a chilled bottle of chardonnay and a six-pack of locally brewed beer. Oh, how Drew was tempted to crack one of those bottles open right now.

"Hey, you're that guy from TV," Aiden said, looking up from the handheld screen. "The one on that sports channel who always yells at the baseball umpires. Coach Chatterson." And just like that, the little boy looked back down at his game, already losing interest.

"Wait, you're *Bobby Chatterson*?" Drew asked as he did a double take at the well-known scruffy red beard and the familiar emblem on his polo shirt. "As in the professional baseball player?"

Drew didn't follow major league sports too much, but even he'd heard of the Hall of Fame pitcher. He could've sworn that Kylie had mentioned her father's name when she'd introduced him, but for some reason—maybe because of his stretched-to-the-breaking-point nerves—Drew's mind hadn't connected those dots.

"You're not a real fast learner, are you, Captain?" Bobby said before giving a knowing side look to Lacey and planting his large frame on the living room couch.

"Dad, Drew's a well-educated psychologist. And he's a lieutenant commander, not a captain," Kylie said. Drew followed her into the kitchen to uncork the wine and help get the meal on the table faster, leaving his guests to linger in the living room.

She looked back to her parents, who were now watching the boys play on the electronic device. "Okay, everyone, dinner is ready. Mom, I know you don't believe in kids not sitting at the table, but Drew and I figured we'd just have the boys eat at the coffee table in the living room so we could talk about, uh—" Kylie coughed as if the words were strangling her "—our marriage."

"Your house, Jellybean, your rules," Bobby said. Drew didn't argue that, technically, it had been Kylie's house for only a couple of hours.

"Maybe next time they can sit with us," Lacey suggested. Drew took the twins' plates to the living room, hoping that there wouldn't be a next time.

"So, Drew, you're a military psychologist?" Mr. Chatterson walked over to the table and sat down before grabbing a large knife.

Kylie had set the chicken out, and looking at the way the large man was already carving off half the bird for himself, Drew's stomach growled painfully at the thought of making do with just salad and rice.

"That's right, sir," Drew said as he took a seat. "I've just been assigned to the Shadowview Military Hospital."

"You must've gone to school a long time for that," Mrs. Chatterson said as she took a sip from her wineglass.

"Well, I joined the navy as a reservist right out of high school. After I finished undergrad, they sent me to the Uniformed Services University of the Health Sciences for my doctorate. I did an internship at Walter Reed before they sent me out with ground forces."

"So what does a military psychologist do?" Bobby asked. "Study psychological warfare and whatnot? Figure out how to play head games with the enemy, that kind of thing?"

"Actually, I specialize in post-traumatic stress disorder. As in how to treat it and how to train other soldiers in recognizing it in themselves and others."

"Huh. Well, I guess they need people for that, too. Personally, I think psychological warfare would be more interesting."

"Really, Dad?" Kylie said. "What do you know about it?"

"Jellybean, I wrote the book on psychological warfare. That's what pitchers do. They sit up on that mound making the batter wonder, 'Is this guy gonna throw a curve ball or is he gonna purposely aim to the left and bean me with a ninety-five-mile-per-hour rocket?'"

Wow, his father-in-law was a world-famous athlete *and* an author. Funny, out of all those books boxed up in the master bedroom, Drew didn't recall seeing any written by major-league relief pitcher Bobby Chatterson.

But Drew tamped down his inner sarcasm and held his tongue throughout the rest of the meal, allowing Kylie's dad to expound on the limitless ways he exercised mind control over his opponents.

Which made Drew wonder if his new in-laws were even the least bit fooled by this whole farce.

Kylie loved her parents to death, but it wasn't until they left that she felt as if she could truly breathe. She finished off the ice cream in her bowl as Drew wiped down the kitchen counters. The boys were watching an animated movie about outer space on television, and Kylie longed to take a hot bath and climb into bed.

In fact, she longed to escape from this total wreck she'd made of her life.

She looked at the rustic simplicity of the cabin and the two pajama-clad children sprawled out on the living room rug. For the next few months, this was her world— a cabin in the woods, a lack of skills in the kitchen and a set of eight-year-old twins who needed some understanding and some structure. She might live in a remote small mountain town in Idaho and she might have been raised with a lovable but overbearing father and four brothers, but she was still a girlie girl.

She didn't do wilderness or cooking.

She liked pedicures and shopping trips and running water, which, thank goodness, she'd found when she spotted the old claw-foot tub in the cabin's single bathroom. So maybe she'd have to move the Lego sailboat and the *Star Wars* figurines out of the way while she relaxed in the bubble bath. She was going to have to get used to moving around a lot of things in her life now.

As Drew finished up in the kitchen, Kylie sneaked away to her room to grab her toiletries and something to sleep in. She locked the bathroom door and ran the water, climbing into the tub before it'd even had a chance to fill up. She dozed off in the water and woke only when she heard a light knock on the door.

"Kylie," Drew whispered. "Is everything okay in there?"

After what he'd witnessed in Reno, he probably thought she was prone to running off and hiding in bathrooms whenever the mood struck her. And maybe she was. "Yes, I'm okay."

"Well, the kids have fallen asleep, and I was going to hit the sack myself. I just wanted to see if you needed anything."

Yeah, she needed a plan. A schedule. If she was going to embark on this crazy pretend lifestyle with Drew and his nephews, she at least needed some sense of organization.

"Hold on." She stood up from the lukewarm water and grabbed the blue towel, since it looked the least used. Step one in her plan was to find out if Drew had a washing machine and start a load of laundry.

Step two. Establish a schedule.

Step three. Find someone to teach her to cook. Kylie'd felt horrible when she realized that a single rotisserie chicken would barely feed her dad, let alone Drew and two growing boys. She should've known better—or at least have paid better attention to how her mom handled cooking for a house full of men. She couldn't do takeout every night and, as cute as the boys were, she wasn't convinced their manners were quite restaurant-worthy yet.

She slipped on a pink tank top and ruffled pajama shorts and exited her temporary sanctuary. Drew was folding blankets in the living room in his own set of pajama bottoms and a snug, faded blue shirt that read Go Navy.

Wait, step one should be to set up some ground rules for how they were supposed to deal with each other and her growing attraction to the man.

"Hey," she said, holding her arms crossed under her chest and then moved them to her hips before returning them to their original position.

Ugh. Why was she so awkward around him? She'd never been so physically attracted to a man. Andrew Gregson made her question every rational thought in her head.

He met her gaze before glancing down her body. She felt her body heat up as though his large, tanned hands were touching her. She cleared her throat and he dragged his gaze back toward hers.

"So, uh, tomorrow," he said. That was all he had to say? Was he going somewhere with this?

"Yep. That's the day after today. What about it?"

He coughed. "Tomorrow I have to report for duty at the hospital, and the boys start their summer day camp."

"Which day camp are they going to?"

"The Junior Crafters. It's the one through the community center."

"Don't you think that one might be a little too juvenile for them?"

"Well, they are juveniles."

"No kidding. What I'm saying is that maybe they need to be in a program that will stimulate them a little more so they'll find less of a need to seek out inappropriate activities."

He tilted his head, and she wondered if she'd already overstepped her role as temporary aunt. "What would you recommend?"

"Alex Russell does a white-water rafting day program for older kids. Maxine's son is enrolled, and the boys seem to look up to Hunter. I think the twins might have more fun there."

"That sounds a little dangerous."

"It's all supervised. And better for them to be rafting, hiking and doing wilderness activities with a professional than to sneak out of the kindergarten-level art class at the community center to see if their basket-weaving projects can float down the river."

"You might have a good point."

"Besides, Alex is good with young boys and runs a tight ship. I have a feeling the teenagers working at the community center won't be able to keep up with Aiden and Caden."

"But is it too late for me to enroll them?"

She tapped her lip, thinking. "I'll tell you what. I'll take them over to Russell Sports in the morning and enroll them. I can also pick them up when I get done with my last client."

"Are you sure?"

"No problem. I might even be able to swing by the market, too. Listen, I'm sorry about not having enough for dinner tonight. I should've been used to how much my dad eats, but for the past few years, I mostly only prepare food for one or else eat out. So this is my late disclaimer that I can help out with the boys and I can help clean, but I'm not much use in the kitchen."

Drew smiled. "I've had roommates who've been less capable."

Did he just call her a roommate?

Of course, that was all she was to him. That and some free babysitting. But it wasn't as if he'd *asked* her to move in. She'd been the one to put them both in this awkward position. And they *still* hadn't clarified things with her parents.

"So if we're all set for tomorrow, I'm going to turn in." She nodded her head toward the bedroom. "Are you sure you don't mind me taking the big bed?"

"Not at all. Sleep well. Let me know if you need anything."

Kylie made her way into the bedroom. She was used to sleeping alone, to living alone. So then why, in this house full of people, did she feel so lonely?

A shrill beeping shook Kylie out of her dream, causing her to roll over and send the biography of Sigmund Freud toppling to the floor. She pushed the screen of her phone, effectively silencing the alarm, and then looked at the fallen book she'd dug out of the boxes to help lure her to sleep last night. It certainly had done the trick.

She listened to the silence as she stretched under the bright homemade quilt. Maybe she should sneak out of her room before anyone else awoke and grab a cup of coffee to help get her through the morning. If today was anything like last night, heaven knew she was going to need it.

She didn't bother getting dressed, figuring she could set up the pod machine she'd brought over from her place and get started on some hazelnut-laced caffeine before hitting the shower.

As she made her way into the kitchen, she saw Drew sitting at the table, an open box of Honey Smacks and a quart of milk beside him.

Maybe she should've put on her robe.

But it wasn't as if he hadn't already seen her in her pajamas last night—or a lot less the morning in Reno. Besides, he must've had the same idea to sneak into the kitchen for a quick breakfast before the chaos of the day began.

"Morning," she said, looking at his faded T-shirt, which stretched across his muscular chest. Seeing his short, spiky hair caused her fingers to twitch. The only things proper looking about Saint Drew at this exact moment were his wire-rimmed glasses. He looked so warm and so masculine and so...

Coffee. She needed coffee, not lustful thoughts about cozying up with her handsome quasi-husband under that king-size quilt.

"Hey," he said simply.

Maybe he wasn't much of a morning person.

But as she plugged in her top-of-the-line brewer and filled it with water, she felt him watching her. A couple of times, while rooting around in the cupboards for where she might've stored her K-Cups, she noticed the tilt in his head as he stared at her. Well, she wasn't much of a morning person, either, and enough was enough.

"Why do you keep looking at me like that?"

"Like what?" he asked, not even straightening up.

"Like you're trying to figure me out."

"Sorry, I can't help it. I slept wrong last night and somehow tweaked my neck."

"Oh, no. I knew that bunk bed was going to be too

small for you. From now on, you're sleeping in the master bedroom."

"Then, where will you sleep?" Her mind flashed to them curled up together on that big bed. "It's not like you're that much shorter than me," he added, and she realized that she'd stepped closer to him, and his head was angled so that he was staring at her long, bare legs.

"Oh, I can sleep anywhere." She walked behind his chair, mostly to put herself out of his line of vision, then felt silly for standing there uselessly. She put her hands to his bare neck and began to massage. "I could sleep on the sofa."

He groaned and leaned toward the table, offering her better access. "I can't very well make a lady sleep on a couch while I'm all cozy in a king-size bed. Besides, what if the twins woke up and found you sleeping in the living room?"

"Then, I'd tell them their uncle is a terrible snorer."

"I'm not, though."

"How do you know you're not?"

"Because nobody that's ever shared a bed with me has complained."

Her hands froze. Whoa. Were they still talking about snoring? Kylie sure hoped so, because the thought of Drew doing anything *but* sleeping in a bed with someone else had her feeling like an upside-down can of whipped cream, ready to discharge.

Speaking of which, an ice cream sundae would really help her cool down right now.

Ugh, she was being ridiculous. Of course he'd slept with other women before. He might've even lived with another woman before.

She forced her fingers to keep moving along the warm

skin of his neck, and before she could change her mind, she asked, "Have you ever been married?"

"What?" He tried to crane his head around to look at her but groaned in pain. "Of course not."

"Ever come close?" Boy, she was really on a roll now.

"You mean, was I ever engaged?"

"Or, you know, living together with a long-term girlfriend? Anything like that?" It was as if she couldn't stop with the personal questions. Thank goodness he couldn't see her face right then.

"I was in a long-term relationship a few years ago, but I don't know how serious it was. I mean, for me at least. She wanted to get married, but I didn't, so we went our separate ways. What about you? Any past boyfriends I need to worry about upsetting because you're suddenly off the market?"

Was she off the market? Obviously she couldn't really date anyone until they got this whole marriage thing resolved. But it was kind of weird to realize just now that her love life was going to be on a temporary hiatus.

"I don't think we'll have any major issues on that front," she said as her hands dipped below the collar of his shirt. She heard him suck in a breath, and thinking he might still be in pain, she wanted to put his mind at ease. "For the next couple of months, I'm all yours."

His shoulders stiffened and he jumped up from his chair, shaking the table and sending cereal and milk sloshing out of his bowl.

"It's fine. I'm fine. My neck's better." His voice was huskier than before, but the angle of his head indicated that she still hadn't worked out the cramp. Had she said something to make him uncomfortable? "I'd better go get dressed before it gets crazy. In here. With the kids waking up and stuff."

Drew jogged toward the bathroom, and it wasn't until she heard the water running that Kylie began to wonder whether it was her personal questions or her intimate touch that had caused such a weird response from the normally cool and reserved psychologist.

It *couldn't* be her touching him. Could it?

Before she could bask in the possibility of her womanly charms, the twins sprinted out of their room and straight for the unattended box of Honey Smacks left behind on the table.

Drew was right. It truly was about to get crazy in here.

After his shower, Drew quickly donned his uniform and left Kylie to deal with the mayhem of getting the kids fed and dressed. Sure, it was the coward's way out, but his hormones were already raging to new heights. It wasn't until he was away from the cabin and driving down the mountain that he allowed himself to revisit that awkward scene in the kitchen this morning.

When he'd seen her long, toned legs in those ridiculously short pajama bottoms, he'd been immediately aroused. Then, as she had begun rubbing his aching neck and making her way to his shoulders, he'd known he was on the edge of losing control. Not to mention, their conversation had taken a sudden intimate turn, and all he could think about was how fabulous her hands were making him feel.

But hearing her say that she was all his was his complete undoing.

How could any male on the planet withstand that kind of temptation? He might've looked like a complete bumbling idiot when he'd knocked over his cereal and raced into the bathroom. But better to be an unsocial fool than to risk pulling her onto his lap and kissing her until neither of them could think straight.

If he wasn't a more disciplined man, he would've done exactly that. And possibly more. But he'd had years of practicing self-control, so he'd gotten the heck out of there.

Last night, they'd decided that Kylie was going to drive Nana's Oldsmobile, since she was dropping off the kids and her Mercedes didn't have enough seat belts, let alone seats, for two extra passengers. The old Jeep his family kept parked at the cabin didn't have an adapter for his iPod so, during his commute, Drew had to listen to the radio. When one of his favorite gym songs came on, he thought about hitting his punching bag later that day, if there was time.

He looked at his crooked pinkie, a reminder of a punch gone astray. He'd taken up boxing when he'd first joined the navy, but by the time he was in graduate school, he'd decided a peaceful and genteel physical outlet would be more suitable. So now Drew's workouts of choice were a combination of yoga and strength training. Controlling his mind and body at the same time usually helped to redirect any of his stress and negative energy.

But today he realized that blasting loud music and boxing might be the only thing that pushed his mind and body to their absolute limits, which wouldn't necessarily soothe him but would allow him to temporarily block out everything else.

He pulled the Jeep into the staff parking lot and turned off the Metallica song before taking a few deep, cleansing breaths and heading into work.

He spent the morning meeting his commanding officer and the hospital chief of staff before being shown into his new office, a beige room near the orthopedic outpatient wing. Some might have thought the psychology department should have been housed in or near the psychiatry unit, but he liked to plan for his team and his patients to be near the physical-therapy rooms. Sure, the issues he dealt with were mental in nature, but he wanted the soldiers who came to him for help to know that their battlefield scars shouldn't be treated any differently or with any more stigma than a physical injury.

If the proximity of his office allowed him better access to the exercise facilities, then that was a bonus. And after seeing Kylie in her skimpy tank top, her pebbled nipples pressing through the thin pink cotton, then feeling her warm, long fingers rubbing along his neck, he needed more than some planking and pikes to get his mind back where it needed to be.

He was organizing his desk when his cell phone vibrated. Drew read the incoming text from Kylie, hoping that getting the kids out the door hadn't proved too much for her.

It took some finagling but I made a deal with Alex Russell to enroll the boys in the adventure camp.

What kind of finagling? And what kind of deal had she promised the owner of the sporting-goods store in order to get special treatment?

Wait. Why did he suddenly care who Kylie was talking to or bartering with? He'd never been jealous in his life. Not even when he'd dated his ex-girlfriend, which probably should've been an early indication that he hadn't been as serious about that relationship as Jessica. He still couldn't believe he'd told Kylie about that this morning. But her question had been simple enough, and really, Drew was pretty curious about Kylie's past, as well.

I'm all yours, she'd said this morning. Even though it

would be unreasonable for him to expect her to give up her dating life temporarily, he didn't like the idea of her ditching him with the twins to go out with another man.

He checked his racing thoughts before he wrote back, Great. How did you swing that?

I told him he could store his camp gear underneath your old boat shed. I also promised to do his quarterly taxes for the next fiscal year.

He let out a breath. Of course she hadn't promised Alex any sexual favors. He wanted to think that Kylie wasn't the type of woman to do something like that. Though honestly, he didn't know what kind of woman she was.

But he didn't like that brief rush of envy that had made its way through his coiled muscles and up into his brain.

Clearly he wasn't thinking straight. Drew rolled his neck, grimacing over the stiff pain still lingering there, then arched his back, stretching out his shoulders. He was hungry. And stressed. Possibly a little tired from trying to sleep all night in a kid-size bed, knowing a sexy and scantily clad redhead, who also happened to be his lawfully wedded wife, was sleeping just a bedroom away from him.

But mostly, he was hungry. Dinner last night had barely filled him up, and this morning's cereal had been left half eaten when he'd made a mad rush for the bathroom to cover up the fact that below the waistband of his pajama pants, his body was reacting way too strongly to Kylie's proximity and touch.

He planned to meet with his new staff at the hospital cafeteria for lunch, but maybe he should tour the building first. Refocus his thoughts. He grabbed the cell phone off his desk, hoping no emergencies would come up for the rest of the day.

At three o'clock, Kylie texted him again, letting him know that she'd picked up the boys from camp and asking him if he needed anything from the grocery store. He remembered her overdone mushy rice and thought about offering to do the cooking tonight, but he was supposed to sit in on a group session that started a few minutes ago and figured he could just call her on the way home.

When he left work for the day, he'd barely gotten his Bluetooth set up when his phone rang. He saw Kylie's name on the display and couldn't answer quickly enough.

"We have a change of plans for dinner tonight," she said by way of greeting. "The microwave caught on fire, and we had a little incident with the fire extinguisher."

He should count his blessings that he'd almost made it a full day without a phone call like this or a trip to the emergency room. "Is everyone okay?"

"Yes, we're fine. The kitchen's a mess and we're trying to air out the cabin since it smells like a chemical explosion at a fishing village."

"How on earth did they set the microwave on fire?"

"Well…uh…it wasn't the boys. It was kinda my fault."

Drew let out his breath, but the sudden thought occurred that Kylie might be covering for his nephews. He gripped the wheel tightly as he wound his way up the mountain and back toward Sugar Falls.

"You see, I was going to try to make a tuna casserole for dinner because Aiden said that was his favorite meal. So we went to the store and got some groceries and I tried to follow a recipe I found online. Then, right when I was about to pull it out of the oven, I realized I forgot to add the tuna."

"Okay," he said when it seemed as if she was waiting for a response. But he still didn't understand exactly what had happened.

"So I figured that I could just heat the tuna up separately and layer it on the top." *Tuna* and *layer* were two words Drew doubted the chefs on the gourmet cooking website used together too often. "Anyway, I threw it in the microwave and then I got busy showing the boys how to separate their laundry and load the washing machine when, *boom*, the whole package burst into flames and smoke started pouring out everywhere."

"Wait. You put an aluminum can in the microwave?"

"Of course not, Drew. I'm not an idiot. It was one of those little pouches that are supposed to be better for the environment, and, well, apparently that has aluminum in it, too. They really should label that kind of thing on their packaging. Anyway, I'm terribly sorry, and I'll buy you a new microwave tomorrow."

He should have taken the time to send her the text offering to cook. "It's fine. Don't worry about it. We can just have plain noodle casserole for dinner."

"Actually, we can't. That's where the fire extinguisher part of the story comes into play."

"What happened to the fire extinguisher?"

"Nothing happened to it. We used it."

"We?"

"Well, not me so much as the boys. I was calling the volunteer fire department, but the twins were smart enough to remember that you kept the extinguisher on the back porch. So they ran and got it and there was a little issue getting it to shoot but… Hey, you know what? We just pulled up, so I'll tell you all about it when you meet us."

"Where are you?"

"Drew, focus." He heard her sigh. "The kitchen is a mess and the casserole was ruined from all the spray. So I brought the kids to Patrelli's for pizza. I'll see you there soon."

She disconnected the call, and Drew didn't know whether to laugh, cry or drive straight to the hardware store for a backup fire extinguisher. Yet one more instance when his perfectly planned life went perfectly wrong. He took a few deep breaths and cranked up the radio. AC/DC was almost done playing by the time he parked the Jeep in front of the Italian restaurant on Snowflake Boulevard.

Chapter Seven

Sugar Falls hadn't changed much since Drew used to come here with his family as a kid. Downtown consisted of a main street lined with old Victorian buildings. Most of the eating establishments and business were on the first floor, with office buildings or private living quarters upstairs. The Sugar Falls Cookie Company was the biggest business in town. Maxine Cooper owned the famous bakery, which was one of the top tourist hot spots on the weekends. She, Cooper and Hunter lived in the renovated apartment above it.

City hall, along with the newly formed police department, was just a couple of blocks down—near Freckles's Cowgirl Up Café. The small town catered to the tourists but during the week, it was mostly just locals hanging out on Snowflake Boulevard. As he walked toward the large oak door under the Patrelli's sign, Drew remembered eating here occasionally when his parents would bring them for the summers. They'd had the best pizza and the newest arcade games.

He stepped into the dimly lit restaurant, and the scent of garlic and yeasty dough told him they probably still had the best pizza. A look toward the arcade in the back told him the games, on the other hand, weren't as new. But the red vinyl booths were full, and the excited kids gathered around the pinball machine and the Pole Position game suggested the patrons came there for the same reasons after all these years.

He spotted his wife immediately and made his way toward her. An older woman wearing an Idaho Steelheads cap stood near the table, looking at the wedding ring on Kylie's finger. Drew's steps slowed, his own left thumb fingering the back of the ring he'd slipped on after Kylie had made that unexpected announcement at the wedding. He wondered if his wife was ashamed of the plain gold bands they'd bought who knew where. Did she wish she had something bigger to show off?

"Drew, this is Mae Johnston." Kylie made the introduction when he arrived. "She's Mayor Johnston's wife. I was just telling her about our...whirlwind courtship."

"It was quite a whirlwind, all right." He smiled and slid into the empty side of the booth, taking Kylie's outstretched hand. Apparently, the pretense was still alive and well.

"I'm glad I'm finally getting the chance to meet you, Doctor. I just think you two are so dang cute together. When you were dancing together at the wedding, I told Cliff you guys looked as in love on that dance floor as we felt on our own honeymoon back in the day."

"How long have you and the mayor been married?" Drew asked, wanting to turn the attention away from his sham of a marriage and that awkward first dance.

"We were only married for a few months that first time. But then we met up again last year at our fiftieth high school reunion, and neither one of us had anything else going on, so we thought, meh, why not?"

"How, uh…romantic?"

"Not really. Now, me and Don—that was my in-between husband—we had us one of those big loves. You know, the kind you read about in stories? But I lost him back in oh-eight. He also had a big romance with bourbon, you know." Mae extended her pinkie out and tipped her thumb toward her lips as though she was drinking out of a bottle. "His ol' liver couldn't take it no more. But me and Cliff make do. Anyway, it was nice getting a chance to meet up with you two. Congratulations."

Mrs. Johnston gave a little wave, then moved on to the next table to make conversation and schmooze. He guessed being married to the mayor, twice, came with certain social duties and civic obligations.

"The boys are in the game room with a stack of quarters, and I ordered you the large meatball sub," Kylie said as she slid a red plastic cup full of soda toward him. "I figured if that wasn't enough, you could share some pizza with us."

"Sounds great," he said and took a big swallow to help appease his stomach, which had begun growling the moment he walked in the door.

"I'm sorry again about dinner. And about your microwave."

A waitress brought out their food, and looking at everything covered in freshly made tomato sauce and piping hot cheese, Drew wrestled with the urge to confess to Kylie that he would have preferred this dinner over tuna noodle casserole any day. It was actually a win-win. "Don't worry about it. You're a whiz with the kids, and you managed to keep them all in one piece today."

"I also negotiated a pretty sweet deal with Alex for their summer camp." Kylie gestured for him to start eating. "Go ahead. The kids will be in there awhile."

"How did their first day go, by the way?" Biting into his toasted sandwich, he let his taste buds get acclimated to what real food was supposed to taste like. A burned-up and oversprayed kitchen was well worth it to savor this kind of heavenly, meaty goodness.

"Actually, Alex said they did pretty well. I guess about halfway through the day, he split them up and assigned them to different wilderness teams, which helped keep them out of trouble."

"Ah, divide and conquer. Why haven't I tried that approach?"

She smiled, and he tried to ignore how natural it felt to talk to her about every day family life.

"My guess is it's easier when there are other kids around to distract them. Plus, it sounds as though they stayed so busy, they didn't have time to get into any scrapes."

"You have no idea how relieved I am that they haven't been kicked out yet."

"Drew, they're sweet boys. Sure, they're a little rambunctious, but they just need some guidance and an outlet for all their energy. Plus, Alex knows he's getting a good deal and will put up with just about anything to get free accounting services from me."

"Kids really aren't my forte," Drew admitted. He also wasn't well trained in having other men indebted to his wife.

"Well, cooking isn't mine. We can't all be perfect, Saint Drew."

"I'll make you a deal. You keep doing what you're doing with the twins, and I'll do all the cooking."

She raised her arms above the red vinyl booth in a sign of victory. "It's a deal. I've waited two hours for you to say those exact words to me. You really know the way to a girl's heart."

Drew motioned toward the mayor, who had just walked up to his wife and greeted her with a playful swat on Mrs. Johnston's rump. "Well, with an example like those two, how can I not try my best to charm you?"

Kylie nodded as she put slices of pepperoni pizza onto plates for the kids. "Just think. If our marriage only lasts a few months this time around, we can always try it again when we turn seventy."

Why in the world had she made that stupid joke about getting married again when they were older? Kylie had been kicking herself all week for saying it. Sure, Drew had chuckled at the time, and luckily the kids had run out of quarters and returned to the table, saving them from any further conversation on the subject.

But a couple of days later, as she sat at her desk, she still wished she could take the words back.

They had settled into a nice routine at the cabin off Sweetwater Bend. Drew usually left for work right about the time the boys woke up. She fed the twins but didn't even have to drive them to Russell's Sports since the day campers now met at the boat shed on the Gregson property, where Alex Russell was storing rafts and kayaks and other river gear. Then Kylie would go to work at her office, a small space she rented above the antiques store on Snowflake Boulevard.

By the time her husband came home in the evenings, the twins were so exhausted from all the hiking, paddling and swimming they'd done during the day, they barely kept their eyes open for dinner—which Drew wasn't much better at cooking than Kylie. Once they got the boys bathed and in bed, he would take off for a couple of hours to do who knew what. She didn't ask him where he was going, but last night she'd sneaked outside and saw that he hadn't actually driven anywhere, which made her realize the light inside the boat shed was on and loud music was coming from the old wooden structure. She wasn't sure what he was doing in there, but at least she was less suspicious that he was off seeing another woman.

Of course, Drew didn't strike her as the kind of man who would cheat on his wife—even a wife in name only. Which made her all the more curious as to what had happened between him and the ex-girlfriend he'd mentioned. He'd said something about the woman being more serious about the relationship than he was, and Kylie had come to the conclusion that Drew didn't like his women getting too clingy.

So she allowed him his space in the evenings and would either read a novel in her room or catch up on all the emails she hadn't gotten to at work. Man, she didn't know how working moms did this kind of thing every day. The twins were fun, but they were a full-time job. Thank goodness it wasn't tax season or there would be no way she could keep this up.

Her phone pinged and she knew it was three o'clock—time to meet the kids. She'd had to set the alarm on Tuesday when she'd gotten so caught up in researching tax code that Alex called her to ask why she hadn't picked Aiden and Caden up from camp yet. Out of four days, she'd forgotten them only once. Not too bad for a new aunt turned surrogate mom overnight.

But tonight was Thursday—her official girls' night out

with her best friends. They'd been meeting every week for the past few years, and she wasn't about to go AWOL now. Although she was settling into her new environment well enough, she would eventually be returning to her real life and needed to try to keep things as normal as possible.

She grabbed her purse and the leather shoulder bag containing her laptop before locking the office door on her way out. As she navigated her way down the steps to the alley behind the antiques store, she fired off a quick text to Drew to let him know about her plans tonight.

She dropped her satchel on the pavement as she fumbled in her designer handbag for the keys to Nana's Oldsmobile. Even though she didn't need the big four-door sedan for kid-hauling purposes since camp drop-off and pickup was now right outside their back door, the rutted driveway to the cabin had seen better days, and she'd gotten her Mercedes stuck in one of the potholes yesterday. So she was back to driving a car that looked like something out of an old episode of *The Brady Bunch*.

She tried to stick the key in the door lock when her purse tipped and half its contents fell on the ground.

"Oh, come on. Would it be too hard to ask for a car with a remote or keyless entry?" she yelled to the empty alley. She decided Drew needed either to pave the road to the cabin or to find her a more updated mode of transportation.

An appreciative whistle came from a passing truck as she bent over to retrieve her belongings. She stood up quickly to yank her skirt down. Maybe it *was* a little too short, now that she was somewhat of a mother figure. While she was used to being on the receiving end of unsolicited pickup lines, she would have been mortified if someone actually hit on her when the twins were with her.

She sat in the Nanamobile, rethinking her entire wardrobe and feeling a decade older already. She envisioned herself dressing like Mrs. Johnston in head-to-toe velour tracksuits, with an old ball cap covering her plain gray hair. If she didn't hit the town tonight with Maxine and Mia, she might as well kiss her thirties goodbye.

Her phone lit up right as she started the engine and she glanced at the screen, but she didn't have time to read Drew's text. Alex told her he was going to charge extra if she came late to pick up the boys again.

When she pulled up beside the cabin, she waved at Alex, who was directing several kids trying to carry man-size kayaks. She reached for her phone and read Drew's message.

I should be home by five ;)

She was frozen in the driver's seat, the engine shut off and a handful of preadolescent boys looking at her as she tried to make heads or tails of the message. Was he flirting with her? Or had he meant to type a smiley face with a wink?

She jumped out of the car, muttered a few words to Alex, waved the kids inside to get them snacks, then got showered and changed.

Drew arrived right on time, but Kylie tried to keep her conversation with him to a minimum—partly because she was still flustered over the text wink and didn't want to read too much into it, which was probably where Drew's ex-girlfriend had gone wrong.

"Are you going to be out late?" He looked pointedly at her jeans and high-heeled boots.

"Not too late, I don't think. It's not as if there's too much nightlife in Sugar Falls."

"Dressed like that, you could generate enough action on your own to last a lifetime."

Before she could ask whether he'd meant his comment as a compliment or a commentary on her fashion sense, the boys ran into the room and launched themselves at her.

"Goodbye hugs!" They both latched on to her, and she squeezed each one three times.

"Is this a new thing?" Drew asked, but he smiled as though he approved of the affection she was showing his nephews.

"Kind of. When I leave for work, it's a little ritual we do." Kylie had started the routine when she realized the boys were clinging a little closer than normal to her on the first day of camp. Surely, with Drew being a psychologist, he could appreciate that the twins might have some issues with separation, especially considering their family history.

"Yeah, Uncle Drew," Aiden said. "You gotta give Aunt Kylie your three biggest hugs so she can think of you at least three times while she's gone."

"Go on, Uncle Drew," Caden added. "Hug her three times."

Drew adjusted his glasses as he looked helplessly at his nephews. Well, it wasn't as if they hadn't touched each other before. And he'd been the one to insist that they keep up appearances even in front of the children.

So she raised her arms and walked toward him. He shrugged before putting his hands lightly on her back and patting her a couple of times.

"No, Uncle Drew. You gotta make them *big* hugs."

"Yeah, like your tightest and best hugs ever."

Drew pulled back and looked down at her. "Three of them, huh?"

She couldn't have been any more embarrassed, so she barely managed a nod. He wrapped his arms tighter, his warm bands of muscles squeezing her until her Italian leather boots were lifted off the floor.

Kylie had no choice but to cling to his shoulders, which reminded her of the last time she'd touched him there. She hoped Drew couldn't tell how damp her palms were.

"One. Two. Three," he counted as he lessened his grip only slightly between each number. "And an extra one for the road so she thinks about me four times tonight."

The boys dissolved into giggles and Drew slowly released her, keeping her body against his until her stiletto heels touched the hardwood floor. It took her a few moments to feel steady enough to stand on her own, let alone walk to the car.

"Okay. Well, goodbye, then." She made the mistake of looking back at him as she wobbled away, and would've traded her favorite pair of designer jeans to know what that parting smile of his meant. She had a feeling she was going to be thinking about Drew way more than four times tonight.

Normally on Thursday nights, she and her girlfriends did an exercise class at Mia's dance studio and then had dinner at a local restaurant. But tonight she really needed to let off steam, so they were bypassing yoga and going directly to the privacy and comfort of Mia's kitchen. Shortly after Cooper had moved into Maxine's apartment over the bakery, he'd begun hosting poker night with some of his new friends, so the women couldn't go there. Thank goodness Mia knew how to cook, because if Kylie had to eat mac and cheese one more time this week, she was going to scream.

Plus, after the massage and the goodbye hug, the physical tension between her and her husband was now reaching an unprecedented level, and she didn't know how to handle it.

Maxine handed her a margarita and a bowl of guacamole as soon as Kylie walked in the door. "We want details," her friend said, foregoing any formal greeting.

She'd given both women brief overviews on Sunday morning as she was packing to move into the cabin, but the updates this week had been vague and via text. "What do you want to know?"

"Like, what were you thinking?" Mia asked first as Kylie plopped onto the kitchen counter stool.

"What's it like living with Doctor Handsome?"

"How's it going being an instant family?"

"How did your dad take the news?"

"Who's doing the cooking?"

The questions came at her rapid-fire, and she couldn't blame her friends their inquisitiveness. If their positions were reversed, she'd be asking the same things. But that last question from Mia brought a halt to the interrogation.

"Really, guys? My whole life is completely upside down and that's what you're worried about? The cooking?"

"Well, it's just that kitchen duty isn't one of your stronger domestic talents," Maxine pointed out. It was a well-known fact.

"But you're great at laundry," Mia said, ever the peacemaker.

"Some claim to fame—I wash a mean load of whites. Which is actually a blessing because living with three extra people, the old washing machine on the back porch never stops running. It's as if my entire day just got three times more stressful. Maxine, I have no idea how you did it as a single mom."

"It was tough, and I only had one little boy. How are you doing with two?"

Kylie sighed. "Actually, not as bad as people might think."

"Who might think that?" Mia turned away from the skillet sizzling on the stove, her face suggesting outrage for anyone who said otherwise. See, this was why Kylie loved her friends. They looked past her outer appearance to the person she really was.

"Come on, you guys know what the town thinks of me. Outrageous and wild Kylie. Great with accounting, horrible with men. Marcia Duncan and Elaine Marconi made it pretty clear at the wedding that they questioned my ability with children."

"But you're great with kids. You do all those pageants with young girls, and your family is huge. Hunter adores you, and you're one of the favorite guest teachers at the Snowflake Dance Academy."

"Hmm." Kylie took a sip of her drink, then pushed it aside in favor of the tortilla chips. "I will say that Aiden and Caden are pretty awesome. They're a little wild, but they are really cute. And funny. It's kind of sad, because they miss their dad and I don't think they really remember their mom. They just need a little structure and some routine, which they got once I enrolled them in Alex Russell's wilderness and adventure camp. And they come home every afternoon exhausted, which is a plus. The kids aren't really the issue here."

Maxine reached toward the chip bowl and pulled it closer to her. "Is the cabin an issue? I know it's pretty remote, but when Cooper lived there for a while, it seemed comfortable and pretty well equipped."

"No, the cabin is fine. I mean, it's a little different than what I'm used to, but you guys know I'm not a snob. Except I will admit that I am absolutely done with that stupid car I got stuck driving. I don't know if I can make it the whole summer motoring around town in the Nanamobile."

"Is that what I saw you driving the other day down Snowflake Boulevard?" Mia asked as she spooned their chicken fajitas onto red pottery-style plates. "I had to take a second look because I thought it was Mae Johnston at first. She has almost the exact same car."

Kylie flinched. Just one week of married life and she was being mistaken for a seventy-year-old woman. And by her best friends, no less.

"So the car situation can be fixed. Just go rent a different one. It's not as if you can't afford it." Maxine's observation was true and not intended as a reference to her family's known wealth. Kylie rarely spoke to anyone about her personal finances, but her friends knew she believed in living strictly off her own income as a CPA—which was fairly substantial considering most of the businesses in town paid her a pretty hefty fee for her services.

Mia put their plates on the small kitchen table. "So if it's not the twins or the cabin, and the car situation can be fixed, it must be Doctor Handsome."

"Stop calling him that," Kylie said as she joined her friends to eat.

"No," Maxine replied as she reached for a warm flour tortilla. "I don't think we will stop. Remember how you used to call Cooper Gunny Heartthrob all the time? Consider this payback."

"But you and Cooper were perfect for each other. And you're the one who said the guy made your heart literally throb when you first met him."

"So you don't think Drew is perfect for you?" Mia asked.

"I don't know if anyone is perfect for me. And trust me,

I've looked far and wide for someone to fit that bill. But more important, I know that *I'm* not perfect for *Drew.*"

"Stop it," Mia said at the same time Maxine argued, "Don't be crazy."

"Ladies, we're talking about Saint Drew here. He looks at me as if I'm a test subject in a psychology experiment."

"No way. I saw the way he was dancing with you at our wedding, and I guarantee you he looked at you as though he wanted to devour you."

"No offense, Max, but you're so crazy in love, all you see are roses and rainbows. Forgive me for thinking your opinion is a little skewed right now."

"Well, I'm not all doped up on pheromones and love," Mia said, referring to her general disillusionment toward most men. "Yet I get the impression that the guy is really into you. How can he not be, Kylie? You're an amazing woman. You're smart, funny, loyal…"

Bless her friends for trying to cheer her up, but they were obviously biased.

"Okay, let's say that Drew possibly *is* physically attracted to me." Which might not be too much of a stretch, considering how she did catch him staring at her sometimes. Or the way he'd hugged her an hour ago. "He's made it clear that this marriage thing is just temporary for the summer. The guy's too straitlaced to want someone like me on a long-term basis. And he's way too proper and polite to act on his attraction."

"So you guys haven't…you know…done anything since that night in Reno?" Mia asked. Her friends knew that Kylie had maintained a tight resolve on her decision to not sleep with a man until she was sure he was The One.

"Ugh. Neither one of us knows if we even did anything back then. I mean, I'm sure we did, because every time I'm in the same room with Drew, my insides get all liquidy and my skin gets tight. I may not know much about sexual attraction, but I'm smart enough to recognize that I can't really control my body when I'm around him. But the not knowing really sucks." Kylie dropped her fork and put her forehead in her hands.

"Oh, honey," Maxine said, and patted her back. "My first time was after the Boise State homecoming game in Bo's dorm room. He hung a sock on the door so none of his fraternity brothers would bother us. It really was the most unromantic night of my life, but every girl deserves to have at least a memory of it. I hate it that you can't re-call yours."

"Why don't you pretend Reno didn't happen and have another first time with him?" Mia asked. "One that you *can* remember."

"Yeah, right." Kylie lifted her head only to find Maxine nodding along. "No. Really, you guys, I can't just re-write history."

"Mia's right. If a column of numbers doesn't add up, you simply erase the answer and start over again. Besides, if you're going to have a do-over, at least you already know that Doctor Handsome is physically compatible with you."

"*Compatible* is a bit of a leap. I said that I was attracted to him. But he's never given me any indication that he wants something more than a roommate."

"Then, why don't you convince him that he does?" Maxine asked.

"How? By seducing him? I can't do that."

"Sure you can."

"Seriously? If I actually made an attempt at it, I'd look stupid, and he'd see right through me. He's trained to read people. Do you have any idea what it's like to live with somebody so calm and in control all the time? Not to mention, I have zero experience in that department, and I'd be a nervous wreck and wind up turning him off completely."

"So you *do* want him," Maxine said triumphantly.

"I never said that." Kylie took a bite out of her fajita, only to have all the seasoned chicken and vegetables fall out the bottom. Ugh.

"You didn't have to say anything. It's written all over your face. You're actually giving this whole seduction idea some thought."

"See? If I'm that obvious to you two, a clinical psychologist is going to figure it out like that." She would have snapped her fingers, but she needed both hands to put her meal back together.

"Let me ask you this." Mia passed her the salsa. "Are you attracted to the man?"

"Obviously. But does that mean I want to have a first-time redo with him? I don't know. We're still strangers. I mean, sure, we're living together, but we really haven't spent that much time together. As soon as he gets home from work, he cooks dinner, we eat and then I get the kids to bed. After that, he takes off for a couple of hours and I crash from exhaustion."

"Wait, did you just say *he* cooks?"

"That may be an overstatement. Maybe I should've said he prepares dinner. Like, he grills the hot dogs or mixes the boxed ingredients together for the macaroni and cheese. There's really little cooking skill involved."

"Still, he's willing to step foot in the kitchen, which shows potential. I say we come up with a plan for you to get him from the kitchen into your bedroom."

Kylie rolled her eyes in frustration. "You think I should sleep with a guy because he knows how to boil noodles?"

"No, we think you should sleep with the man because

you're obviously attracted to him and could use a little spark in your life." Maxine winked at her.

"You guys know good and well that I have no business seducing anyone. Especially when I have no idea what his feelings are on the issue."

"Have you thought about asking him?" Mia asked.

"Of course I have. But we're never alone together."

"Good point," Maxine said. "It's not as if you can ask him in front of the twins. Okay, forget the whole seduction thing. But you definitely need to get him alone so you guys can hash everything out. Here's what I'm thinking…"

Drew got the okay from Cooper to bring the boys to hang out with Hunter at poker night while Kylie was out with her friends. Besides Monday's dinner at Patrelli's, he'd just eaten the best meal he'd had all week. Who knew such a tough and quiet Marine turned police chief could be such an amazing cook? He'd need to get his friend's recipe for chicken-fried steak and show Kylie that he could bring a little more to the table. Literally.

She was doing so much around the house with the boys, and all he seemed capable of was going to work and making dinner. But even his meal efforts left much to be desired. Maybe that was why she'd been in such a hurry to get out for the night. But did she have to dress as if she was on her way to a modeling shoot? He hadn't been able to stop looking at her long legs in those jeans…

He'd felt like such a dope after that goodbye-hug stunt. He'd done it because his nephews were watching and seemed to expect it. Plus, he'd known how important it was for children to have a sense of routine, and he should've expected the boys to have some separation-anxiety issues.

But he didn't know how much more of this fake physical affection he could take. When he'd felt Kylie fully pressed up against him, he hadn't wanted to let her go. She must think he was the world's biggest walking hormone, because she'd practically flown out the door the second he'd released her.

"So how's married life treating you?" Thankfully, Cooper had waited until after the boys went back to Hunter's room to play video games to ask the question.

Alex was shuffling the cards, and Drew thought the man seemed overly eager to hear his response. It wasn't the first time he'd wondered if the outdoorsman was interested in his wife.

See, there he went again, thinking of Kylie as his real wife. But it was just so easy to do. They'd fallen into a comfortable domestic pattern, and she was amazing with his nephews. Heck, she was amazing in general. But it wasn't as if what they had would last much longer than this summer. In fact, after the way she'd nearly torn the transmission out of her sports car as she'd hauled down the bumpy driveway in an effort to leave tonight, he wondered if they'd even last another week.

"It's going all right," Drew said, not wanting to give up much information, but knowing the cop was going to keep asking until he got the answers he wanted. "It's only been a few days, so we're still establishing a routine."

"Are you guys getting to know each other pretty well?" Cooper didn't have to remind anyone that Drew had met his wife less than two weeks ago.

"It's a process." Okay, maybe that was a stretch. He hadn't been able to stay in a room alone with her long enough to learn much. He could tell she had a great heart, she adored the kids and she took her job seriously. But everything he'd assessed came from analysis at a distance. It wasn't as if they were at the stage where they could ask each other personal questions. Or have meaningful conversations about what they wanted out of life. Probably because every time he looked at her, he envisioned her in her skimpy pajamas—or worse, nothing at all—and his head would cloud up with lust to the point that he had to do something to burn up the sexual energy building inside him.

When he folded for the fourth time that night, his two buddies exchanged a look.

"How's that punching bag I set up in the boat shed working for you?" Alex asked.

"It's pretty good. I've tried a few yoga classes at the hospital during lunch, but I've been going out to the shed and doing some hitting for a couple of hours every night after the kids go to bed."

"A couple of *hours*?" Alex asked, incredulous.

"Every *night*?" Cooper followed.

"Yep. It helps me unwind." The two men exchanged another look. "What?"

"Well, if I had a woman who looked like Kylie in my bed," Alex said, "I could think of a lot more enjoyable ways to unwind than punching some bag in an old, drafty boat shed."

"Well, you don't have *my wife* in your bed, and I'd appreciate it if you would refrain from speculating what it would be like if you did."

"Whoa, Saint Drew. Is this jealousy I'm sensing?" Cooper was doing that blasted smirking thing again. "That's not very Zen of you. Maybe you need to stop boxing and focus more on your yoga classes."

"I'm not jealous." But even Drew knew the statement was a lie.

"Listen, man, I meant no offense." Poor Alex. He really hadn't said anything that most red-blooded males wouldn't have been thinking. Drew did have a beautiful woman sleeping in the room next to him, and perhaps he was on edge because there wasn't a thing he could do about it.

"I'm sorry, guys. It's just been really stressful with the new job, and I'm still not used to taking care of the twins. Then this whole business with Kylie is somewhat unexpected territory."

"Hey," Alex said. "Don't worry about it. When Cooper was falling love with Maxine, he was an absolute bear to those poor boys on our Little League team. He would make them run bases just for looking at him sideways."

"I'm hardly falling in love with Kylie." Drew tried to laugh but threw down his cards instead. Man, he sucked at poker.

"Yeah, that's what Cooper thought when it happened to him." Alex drew two more cards.

"If you want some advice," Cooper said, matching the four cookies already in the pile on the center of the table, "things will probably go easier for you if you just let go of all that stupid control you're used to and enjoy getting to know her."

"I'm a licensed psychologist, you know. I don't think I need marriage counseling from a guy who is using his new wife's bakery inventory as poker chips."

"Hey, we all win when Maxine's cookies are used for bartering. And right now, I'm ahead three chocolate chips and four maple pecans."

Alex was eating his winnings, so there was no way to know for sure who was really ahead.

"Are you guys going to the Marconis' costume party this weekend?" Cooper changed the subject.

Chapter Eight

Drew couldn't believe it was already Saturday night—the one-week anniversary of the unexpected announcement of their marriage. And they were once again venturing out into public. He looked in the bathroom mirror at his makeshift costume. He was an educated man, but he had absolutely no idea what a bedroom sheet had to do with a grown man's birthday party.

"Hey, Kylie," he called out to the woman with whom he now shared a house and kid-raising responsibilities, but absolutely nothing else. "Why do I have to wear this thing again?"

She squeezed into the small bathroom and stood behind him. Through the reflection in the mirror, he took in her oversize hot pink fluffy bathrobe as she repleated the bed linen over his shoulder. She was always doing little stuff like this for the boys and around the house, making things in their lives better, smoother.

A guy could get used to that kind of treatment...

"I told you," she said as though patiently explaining herself to a child. "The Marconis have a big celebration every year for Chuck's birthday. A few years ago, people started wearing themed costumes to the party. Well, Sugar Falls residents do not like to miss an opportunity to dress up—you should see the town on Halloween."

But it wasn't Halloween and Drew wasn't one to play make-believe. He tried not to tense as her long fingers grazed his skin under the white fabric of his homemade gladiator costume.

Her hand stilled on his shoulder, and he caught her expression in the mirror. She was looking toward his lower back, and he remembered the last time they had been in the same room wearing nothing but the linens from the hotel room bed and her lacy underwear...

"Maybe I should put a shirt or something underneath this." He wasn't feeling particularly cold. In fact, the temperature in here seemed to be rising. And a small part of him wanted her to comment on his appearance.

"Maybe," she replied, her voice sounding huskier than normal.

He turned toward her, but her gaze remained below his shoulders. He tipped her head up, and his breath caught when he saw the heat in her eyes. His finger stroked her chin, and she leaned her face closer to his.

But before he could claim her full lips, the bathroom door slammed into him. "Aunt Kylie, are you *sure* that no other boys are going to be dressed as a two-headed Jabba the Hutt?" Caden asked, his brother squirming beside him under mounds of green fabric.

The woman Drew had been about to kiss jumped back and gave her full attention to his nephews, breaking the intimate spell.

"Well, if there are, they won't be as big as you two."
Kylie caught Drew's eyes in the mirror. He had to give her
credit for the brilliant idea of pairing the boys up in a joint
costume that would keep them attached to each other and
easier to locate in a crowd.

"Okay, but can we have light sabers, too?" Aiden asked
as she escorted the twins out of the bathroom.

Drew braced one hand on the counter, steadying his body
and then steadying his breathing. That had been close. He
took off his glasses and splashed some cold water on his
face. If it hadn't been for him leaving the cabin every night
to work off some tension, this week would've been filled
with a whole lot more dangerous moments like that one.

And that would've been so unfair to both of them. Not
only because of the commitment he'd made to himself
not to get involved with another woman until he was sure
that she was The One, but also because Kylie was such a
kindhearted person, she deserved to have that knight in
shining armor she'd admitted to dreaming about. This charade was meant to last only the summer, but if they took
things to a physical level, he didn't know if he would be
capable of letting go.

It was like Icarus flying too close to the sun. He was
dying to touch the warm and vibrant woman who was
his wife but was too afraid that once he did, his defenses
would melt and he would spiral out of control.

"C'mon, Uncle Drew," a voice called out from the living room. "We're gonna be late."

He took one last look in the mirror, then followed his
temporary family out to the car. Kylie didn't make eye
contact with him the entire drive over to the Marconis'.
Drew wondered if she was tense about seeing Elaine since
the woman had insulted her last week, or if she was thinking about what had almost happened between them just

now. Luckily, the boys chattered nonstop in the backseat, oblivious to the silent adults in front of them.

Apparently Kylie had been right about this party. It was one of the more popular events of the year. So popular, in fact, they had to park a few blocks away. The partygoers walking toward the Marconis' restored Victorian home off Snowflake Boulevard were dressed in similar attire.

"There are Hunter and Cooper," Aiden shouted, pointing at what appeared to be Gandalf and Frodo. At least Drew wasn't the only grown man here not wearing pants. The boys jumped out of the car the second Drew put it in Park and ran toward their new friend and his stepdad.

Kylie was still sitting in the front seat, messing with her pink robe, so he exited and called out to the police chief, who waved and pointed two fingers to his eyes, acknowledging that Cooper would watch the twins. Drew straightened his costume as he walked over to her side of the vehicle.

When she finally emerged, his chest almost exploded from his sudden intake of air.

She was dressed in a short, white, gauzy skirt that barely covered her perfectly curvaceous rear end. A snug corset trimmed in gold pushed against her full breasts. Her legs were bare except for the straps of her sandals, which wrapped all the way up to her knees.

"What are you wearing?" He tried to keep the shock from his voice, but his heart rate was wreaking havoc on his brain function.

She looked down at her figure, then tilted her head. "A costume?"

"That is *not* a costume. I've seen bathing suits with more material."

"Well, technically, I'm supposed to be Diana, goddess of the hunt."

The only thing she could possibly be hunting for in that getup was men. A green haze clouded over his eyes, and he tried to dismiss the alien emotion he'd been experiencing all week.

"You should probably put that robe back on." He reached past her to open the car door and grab something, anything, with which to cover her up.

"Why? It's not going to be cold once we get inside, and I don't want to leave it behind accidentally. It's my favorite robe."

If it was truly her favorite, then why hadn't he seen her wear it since she'd moved into the cabin? Instead, she'd paraded around the place in those skimpy pajamas that had him racing out to the boat shed to exercise and clear his mind.

"But your outfit is a bit too..." How did he put this delicately without revealing his jealousy? Or sounding like a complete prude?

"A bit what?" Uh-oh. She was standing up straighter, and he'd seen that defiant look in her eye before. She was like that Amazon queen back in their hotel room, ready to do battle.

"What I'm trying to say is that your outfit might draw too much attention."

"I'm used to being stared at. Don't worry. It doesn't bother me."

"I'm not worried about it bothering *you*. I don't like the way it's bothering *me*!"

"I thought nothing rattled you, Saint Drew."

He planted his hands on his hips so he wouldn't be tempted to show her just how completely rattled he actually was. He would've shoved them into his pockets if he'd had any. "Well, right now that skimpy costume is doing a pretty good job of it."

"How can my outfit possibly affect you?"

Oh, there were plenty of ways it was affecting him right this second. But he wouldn't admit that. Instead, he said, "I'm more concerned about the way it's going to affect the other men at the party." Well, that was partially honest.

She looked genuinely confused, almost as though she didn't realize how powerful her appearance was. "Drew, I like how I look and I like what I wear. I dress for myself. Not for you, not for the uptight busybodies in this town and definitely not for the men."

He couldn't believe she didn't understand what he was trying to tell her. "But the men will still be looking at you."

"Why can't they look at me?"

"Because you're *my* wife."

And as if to sear his brand on her, he snaked his arm around her waist and pulled her toward him, dipping his head to press his lips to hers. She startled in surprise, and he took advantage of the opportunity by brushing his tongue along her slightly opened mouth. Fire shot through him the moment her tongue tentatively met his, and he pulled her tighter against his body.

The satin-covered wires of her corset dug into the side of his chest that had been left bare, and it was all he could do to not tear the ridiculous garment off her and feel her soft skin against his.

She wrapped her arms around his neck and leaned in closer, her desire matching his own.

His body had wanted this from the moment he'd seen her standing in the hotel room in Reno. And finally, he was giving in to what his brain and his conscience had been denying him. He let his hands wander down past her waist and over the curve of her bottom. He pulled her hips closer to him. Just for a second, he thought. Just long enough to ease the aching arousal beneath his gladiator costume.

She was so tall that even standing up, she nestled against him perfectly, and he knew that the mere pressure would never be enough.

He wanted her.

He needed her.

And if he wasn't careful, he'd have her—right here against the door of Nana's Oldsmobile.

The thought should have sobered him, but her moan only incited his passion, and he was immune to any rational thought. He'd been right. One touch, one taste of Kylie would never be enough.

It wasn't until she pulled back and urgently spoke his name that Drew realized they weren't alone. He'd been so caught up in their kiss, in her, that his senses had tuned out the rest of the world.

"Are you two going to come inside and join the party?" Cessy Walker asked when Drew regained enough control to release his wife and what was barely covered by her minuscule skirt.

"From the looks of things, I'd say you lovebirds were creating your own party out here." Freckles's laugh threatened to pop a few sequins off her wicked-witch ensemble.

"You ladies go on ahead. We'll be right behind you," Kylie said, her voice not quite as shaky as Drew's would have been—had he been able to find it.

"Sure you will." Cessy, dressed in Glinda's pink ball gown and tall crown, shot them a disapproving look as Freckles sang the chorus from "When a Man Loves a Woman." The women walked on, their costumes a direct contrast to their personalities.

Drew clenched his jaw. He was ashamed. And speechless.

This wasn't him. This wasn't how he acted. His parents had raised him better than this. Yet he was behaving like a sex-starved maniac, treating Kylie as though she was some cheap hussy in a back alley. This was why he didn't let himself lose control—why he'd spent years studying the mind and its cognitive functions. This was why he'd had to redirect and distract himself physically every night this past week by working out.

He didn't look at Kylie. He couldn't bear to see her embarrassment—or worse, her disgust—at finding out she was married to an absolute ogre who couldn't even put a lid on his lustful urges when they were out in public.

"We should probably make our way to the party," she said.

He should have been relieved she wasn't asking him to drive her home. Of course, after the behavior he'd just exhibited, it was wise of her to not get into a car alone with him. She probably wanted to be as close to other witnesses as possible.

He chanced a peek at her and saw her adjusting her corset and using the side mirror to fix her smeared lip gloss. "I'm so very sorry." It was the first response that came to him.

"There's nothing to be sorry about," she said, starting to walk down the street.

He caught up to her. "I know you probably would prefer to forget what just happened. But I just wanted to make it clear that I know it was wrong and I promise nothing like that will ever happen again."

Her steps quickened, but otherwise, Kylie gave no indication that she'd heard him, let alone believed him.

"It was bad enough your former mother-in-law caught us making out like a couple of teenagers," Kylie whispered to Maxine in a corner of the Marconis' lit garden. The party had spilled from the hosts' elegantly restored

Victorian mansion and into their yard, but she was too
twisted up inside to enjoy the twinkling lights or the professional catering. "But then he told me that kissing each
other was wrong. I told you this plan would never work."

"Kylie," Mia said, joining them. "I just saw your husband pacing over by the buffet table like a lion trapped
in a cage. Every time someone comes up to him to congratulate him on his marriage, he goes straight for the
bacon-wrapped scallops and crab cakes. I know the cooking situation at home isn't ideal, but if he keeps downing
the seafood appetizers like that, he'll wind up with a stom-
achache and tonight will be ruined."

"Stop worrying, you two," Maxine said. "Mia, the plan
is actually going better than we expected. Doctor Handsome got all worked up when he first saw Kylie in her
costume outside, and they got busted getting all hot and
heavy against the Nanamobile."

"Eww!" The dance instructor scrunched her nose.

"Don't worry. He only kissed me to prove a point. Then
he apologized and promised it would never happen again."

"But how was the kiss?"

"It was fine." She tried to focus on the other guests and
feign an interest in the party. But she knew her friends
weren't buying it. "Okay, so it was wonderful. Beyond
wonderful. I've never been kissed like that before, and
if Cessy and Freckles hadn't walked by when they did, I
doubt we would ever have made it inside."

"You guys got busted by Mrs. Walker? Double eww."

"Thanks." Kylie crossed her arms in front of her, wanting to duck farther into the corner. "That makes me feel
way less mortified about the situation."

"Sorry," Mia said, putting her arm around Kylie.
"Maybe we need to restrategize."

"I don't think so." Maxine nodded toward Drew. "See

how he's staring at Chuck Marconi and the rest of the good ol' boys club holding court over by the open bar?"

"Hmm." Kylie glanced at her husband, who didn't look at all like his normally poised self. "I wonder what they did to get him all bent out of shape."

"Kylie, he's giving them the evil eye because those men are all gawking at you and your costume."

"First of all, my costume is not that bad. There are other women here with outfits similar to mine."

"Yeah, but those women are working with a lot smaller curves than you."

She rolled her eyes. It wasn't as if she could help the way her body was shaped. "Second of all, if you think he's upset because they're looking at me, you're seriously..."

She lost all sense of what she was about to say because the subject of their conversation was striding toward her, looking more like a Special Forces sniper than a scholarly navy psychologist. She swallowed and glanced at her friends, hoping for some sort of support. But they were just standing there with silly grins on their faces.

"Drew, how are you?" Maxine said when he arrived, seemingly ready to pounce. "We were just talking about Kylie's costume and how beautiful she looks in it."

"*Beautiful* is one way to describe it." He glanced over his shoulder at the men by the bar, then stood closer to Kylie, as if he was trying to block her from their view.

What had gotten into him? When she'd chosen her outfit, she'd had no intention of trying to make him jealous. She'd simply wanted him to see her in a sexier light. Or at least draw his physical interest. "Seriously, you guys. Stop giving me a hard time. I'm supposed to be Diana. You know, the Greek goddess of the hunt?"

"Wasn't Diana also the goddess of fertility?" Mia

murmured before Maxine nudged her in the ribs. Kylie frowned at her friends.

"Anyway, Drew," Maxine said, "did Kylie tell you that Hunter invited the twins to come stay the night at our place tonight?"

"Ah, no. I'm pretty sure that never came up," he said, finally dragging his attention away from the group at the bar. "I don't think the boys are ready to handle a sleepover just yet. They're still getting used to being with me and, even though they're settling into a routine, I don't know if I trust them not to be a handful for you."

He was putting the brakes on this whole time-alone thing, and Kylie couldn't help but suspect he was doing so wittingly. He didn't want to be alone with her tonight and knew that if he allowed the twins to stay with Maxine and Cooper, he'd lose his towheaded buffers.

"Of course they won't be a handful. And we'd love to have them. I can understand you worrying about them spending the night somewhere new. I was the same way with Hunter the first time he went to a sleepover. But I promise that Cooper and I will take good care of them, and we'll even make extra pecan waffles in the morning for you when you come pick them up."

"Are you sure?" he asked, and Kylie's pulse took a little leap. She didn't want to think that the only reason he was relenting was the promise of another home-cooked meal. But when he looked at her, one eyebrow raised as if to ask her opinion, she couldn't help but hope he was silently asking her if she was comfortable with the arrangement.

She honestly didn't know if she was. But she *did* know they couldn't continue living together and pretending the kiss of the century hadn't just happened. She gave a tentative nod, hoping they could use the kid-free opportunity to have a good, long talk and sort out their feelings—or at least set some ground rules for the rest of the summer.

After several rather transparent reassurances from Maxine, Drew went to speak to the boys, and she could hear the children's squeals from across the yard. Part of her wanted to squeal as well, but the other part of her wanted to run straight to the Nanamobile and drive directly to Noodie's. She'd never needed some serious ice cream therapy more than she did at this exact moment.

Saying their goodbyes and doing their three hugs—with two excited kids in one oversize costume—created enough of a scene without her having to wonder if every townsperson home was snickering about why the newlyweds were leaving early.

Her husband was perfectly polite—as usual—but did not touch her as they walked back to the car. He opened the door for her and she thanked him, but otherwise they didn't speak. She was too afraid he might suggest dropping her off at her condo—with her brother, who'd been as surly as a grizzly bear when she'd talked to him a few days ago.

Instead, she repeated prime factors in her mind until he turned onto Sweetwater Bend. Apparently, he was taking her back to the cabin. She didn't know whether to exhale the breath she'd been holding or to start sucking in more air to prevent her from hyperventilating.

"I always forget how beautiful the stars are up on this mountain," he said, finally breaking their uncomfortable silence.

She craned her head, leaning forward to see out the windshield. "I think it's because the air is so pure up here."

See, they were making small talk. She could do this.

"My brother, Luke, the twins' dad, used to say that the

sky was better in Sugar Falls than anywhere else in the world because it was so close to heaven."

"Do you miss your brother?" There, that was a neutral enough subject.

"I do. We're twins, so we have this connection—I don't know how to explain it. Sometimes, when we're not together, I feel things as though I'm experiencing them with him."

"Is he anything like you?"

Drew chuckled. "Hardly. My mom would say we're exactly alike when it comes to certain things, but mostly, we're complete opposites. Luke is way more intense and impulsive. He knows what he wants and he goes after it. I'm more of a thinker, a planner. I manage my emotions better than he does, which is why we went into such different fields."

Kylie didn't want to point out that just a couple of hours ago, Drew certainly hadn't managed his emotions all that well. And she'd been enjoying it.

"He was the fun twin growing up," he continued. "The wild one. I was the dependable son. I always went out of my way to follow the rules, as though my perfect behavior would offset his recklessness. When he married the twins' mom, he became a little more like me—methodical, but still passionate about life. I know it sounds weird, but back then a part of me thought that if matrimony made him more like me, then maybe finding a wife of my own would make me more exciting like him."

"So then why didn't you marry your last girlfriend?" This was the kind of conversation they should be having on date number two, not on the second week of marriage. He'd touched on his prior relationship before, but now Kylie was wondering exactly what Drew was looking for in a wife.

He turned onto the private dirt road toward the cabin, and she wanted to tell him to keep driving. To keep talking.

"I don't know. I dated Jessica for a few years, but it just never felt right."

Wait. Did he say a few *years*?

He parked the car and shut off the engine. Kylie wanted to ask him if this moment together felt right. If *she* felt right. But the man had just admitted that it had taken him a hell of a lot longer than two weeks to decide if a woman was the one. Besides, on this night of all nights, she didn't want him comparing her to his ex. Or to any other women.

She needed him to realize that she was special. That she was unique and that she'd already given him something sacred that she'd never given another man. Even if neither one of them could remember it. Tonight's conversation had to be about just the two of them, because she didn't know how long she'd have him in her life, and she wanted to know that what they had—even if it was only temporary—was meaningful.

He rested his arm along the back of her seat and turned to look at her. Maybe it took Drew years to figure out his feelings, but apparently Kylie was making quick work of hers. No doubt that if he looked at her this way two weeks ago, even without the cocktails in souvenir cups, she would've had a hard time staying away from him.

"Listen," he said, keeping his hand nearby but not touching her. "I just wanted to apologize again for my behavior earlier."

Whoa. There he went with his stupid regrets again. "I told you that you had nothing to be sorry for."

She shoved open her door and then slammed it closed behind her—no small feat considering it had to be two hundred pounds of solid steel. She was stomping up the steps to the back porch when he called after her.

"If I shouldn't be apologizing, then why are you so clearly upset?"

"I'm not upset." Disappointed? Yes. Humiliated? Totally. She stormed into the cabin with him close on her sandaled heels.

"Really? Because I'm pretty sure I'm the expert on recognizing people's emotions."

"Well, Doctor Perfect, you certainly aren't the expert on me." She threw her small gold clutch on the table and turned to face him, ready for the showdown. How dare he presume to know how it felt to have the sainted Andrew Gregson regret their kiss? To have him vow not to make the same mistake with her twice?

"Kylie, I think we need to address this. I don't want you to feel uncomfortable or worry that I can't control myself around you."

"Drew, has it ever dawned on your expert mind that I don't *want* you to control yourself around me?"

She could hear the air hiss between his clenched teeth.

"Then, you'd better be really sure about what you *do* want, Kylie, because as you saw before we went inside the party, once I get close to you, I don't know if I'll be able to stop."

It took every bit of courage she possessed to put one foot in front of the other and walk toward him. This was it. There'd be no going back now. "I don't want you to stop."

Chapter Nine

Before Kylie could take that final step, Drew came toward her, placing one hand on her cheek a split second before molding his lips against hers. She knew the kiss they'd shared a couple of hours ago had shaken her senseless, but she'd never imagined a man could make her feel like *this*.

As though she was melting, yet she couldn't get warm enough.

For a guy who always practiced such an unusual amount of caution, he was certainly leaving her no opportunity for second-guessing and no time for doubt. And she didn't mind one bit, because she'd never been more certain of anything in her life. His mouth delved farther into her own as he drew her body closer. His fingers tangled into her long auburn hair, keeping her head exactly where he wanted it.

His chest was chiseled, hard as rock, and she ran her hands along its ridges, amazed that something so firm could also be so hot. The upper section of his homemade costume had come unpinned, and she felt even more heat as his exposed skin pressed against the flesh rising above her corset. He must have felt the same heat, because his fingers were immediately at her back, working the small stays that barely managed to hold her top closed.

Drew didn't show the slightest hint of slowing down, and Kylie worried that she'd soon be topless in the living room. This might not be her first time with him, but it was the first time she would be able to remember the experience, and she didn't want it occurring out in the open.

"Should we go into the bedroom?" she murmured against his lips. His response was to move his hands to cup her bottom and then lift her up, forcing her to wrap her long legs around his waist.

She was pretty sure that he carried her to the king-size bed. But by the time he laid her down, she didn't care how she'd gotten there, only that she didn't want him to let her go.

His mouth never left hers as he tore what remained of her corset and flung it to the ground. His large hands covered her breasts and she arched into him, unfamiliar with the sensation, yet craving more.

She had never been ashamed of her body, but suddenly she was hyperaware of everything he was doing to it and wondering if her response was normal. How could she experience this sense of floating above the bed when his tall, golden body was planted so firmly above her?

He balanced himself on one arm, kissing a trail down to her tightened nipples, as he used his other hand to slide her skirt and panties past her hips. When he brought his fingers back up, he did so along her inner thigh. The metal of his wedding band was cool against the delicate skin near her core, and she couldn't help but think, *This man is my husband. I'm finally giving myself to my husband.*

He was passionate and he was perfect and he was hers, just as much as she was now his.

She reached for his head and pulled his lips back to hers, wanting to seal her realization with a kiss. The movement caused his body to wedge itself between her open legs and, without hesitation, he drove into her. Her muscles clenched and she stilled, the small burst of pain already ebbing away.

He pulled back and looked at her face. "You're a... You've never... We've never?" There was no accusation in his blue eyes, only tenderness.

"I guess that answers the question of whether or not we already did this in Reno," she said, not sure of what she should do now. All she knew was that she didn't want to ruin this beautiful moment with any recriminations. She shifted her hips and his shaft slid deeper inside her.

He buried his face against her neck and said, "Forgive me, honey, but I can't stop."

"I don't want you to."

He groaned before slowing his pace long enough for her to meet his rhythm. She moaned as the pressure built inside her. When she wrapped her legs around him to draw him in even farther, the dark room went brighter. Then the light exploded into a thousand tiny fragments right as he called out her name.

Drew held Kylie close to him even as he cursed himself. He was an animal. A monster. He'd taken his wife's virginity and hadn't been able to control himself long enough to ensure she wasn't hurt.

"I'm sorry for not being more gentle," he said, while hoping she wasn't too sore. He didn't want to cause her pain, but she felt so perfect in his arms, he didn't think he could wait to have her again.

"I thought you weren't supposed to apologize anymore."

"That was before I knew you were a… That you'd never done this before."

"It was perfect. I wouldn't have wanted you to change a single thing." She snuggled in closer to him, and he felt her breath warm against his neck.

The woman was incredible.

When their breathing had slowed to a normal pace, she stretched, then sat up on the bed, pulling the quilt in front of her and up under her arms.

He reached for his glasses on the nightstand but couldn't find them. "Where are you going?"

"To get my robe."

"Like that? I think it's still out in the car." He stroked his hand down her bare back. He knew she'd said otherwise, but he worried her newfound modesty was due to the way he'd just ravished her. When she turned her head toward him, her long auburn curls fell around her creamy shoulders, and she smiled at him. His stomach flipped over.

At least he thought it was a smile. He couldn't be sure without his glasses.

"I guess I'll have to stay like this until morning."

"I don't mind if you don't," Drew said as he tugged on the quilt, using it to pull her back into his arms.

She came willingly and he tried to command himself to go slow, to be gentle. But any thoughts of her still being tender were a distant memory as his passion once again took over his brain. They made love a second time and then collapsed in each other's arms. The quilt was nowhere to be found and the sheets were in a tangled heap at the foot of the bed.

But Drew didn't care. His body was still burning and he didn't need anything but Kylie to keep him warm.

He awoke to the sun streaming through the bedroom window and the smell of Kylie's shampoo tickling his nose. Using his free arm, he tried not to wake her as he reached for his glasses, this time determined to see his wife in all her splendid glory.

But he couldn't find the wire frames, or even feel the sturdy oak table that was usually pushed up against the bed. He squinted at the room, and his blurry eyes landed on the nightstand, which had somehow toppled over onto its side, several feet away.

How in the world had that happened?

He ran his fingers through his hair, careful not to disturb Kylie, who was sleeping soundly, pressed up against his side. He hadn't been with a woman since Jessica, and during that time, he'd never experienced the uninhibited reckless abandon he'd felt last night. Honestly, he'd never experienced anything like that before with anyone.

His cell phone chimed, the low decibels indicating it was coming from the other room. He thought about the possibility of an emergency and gently disengaged his arm from under her shoulders. He almost stepped on his discarded glasses before picking them up off the floor and walking naked into the living room.

"Hello?" he whispered into the phone, only to realize Kylie'd followed him out. And apparently she'd found the bed cover, because she was wrapped up in it.

"Hey, Uncle Drew," one of his nephews responded. "Chief Cooper is making waffles and wants to know if you and Aunt Kylie are coming for breakfast."

"I…uh…don't know."

"Is everything okay with the boys?" she asked.

He put his hand over the mouthpiece. "They want to know if we're coming over for waffles."

"Are they making the pecan ones where he uses the maple-cream-cheese glaze?"

He relayed her question to his nephew and waited for the response. But seeing her in the living room, barely covered, her hair all wild and tousled from their love-making, Drew suddenly didn't feel so hungry—at least not for breakfast.

The little voice came back on the line. "He said yes, although me and Aiden don't want no nuts, so he's gonna make ours plain. But he's also making bacon and scrambled eggs."

Drew's stomach growled and he nodded at Kylie, conveying the information.

"Tell them we'll be there in twenty minutes," she said.

He disconnected the phone, calculating how far downtown was from the cabin. She certainly hadn't left them very much time. He walked toward her, and it wasn't until she looked down and then up again that he remembered he was completely nude.

She bit her lower lip and he asked, "Are you sure you're in such a hurry to leave?"

"Well, he *did* say bacon and..."

He interrupted her by kissing the column of her neck. Man, she had smooth skin. He traced a finger along her shoulder, then toward the edge of the quilt, right where her breasts were rising above the fabric.

"Are you terribly hungry?" he asked.

"Starving." She dropped the bedding to the floor before rising up on her tiptoes to meet his lips.

Thirty minutes later, they were still naked and still in the living room, stretched out on the discarded blanket and once again trying to catch their breath.

"We should probably act like responsible adults and go pick up the children." She spoke first. She was smiling, but Drew hated the reminder that he had again lost all control and rational sense.

"You're right." He should apologize, but he wasn't feeling very sorry. In fact, he was feeling quite the opposite. He was glad they'd made love and he was looking forward to doing so again.

"I wonder if they'll have any food left by the time we get there." She walked toward the bathroom, twisting her hair up into a bun on top of her head, and he was tempted to follow her into the shower.

But she closed the door behind her and he thought she was already transitioning into modesty mode. Perhaps she already regretted what they'd done. He walked to the bedroom, stripping off the sheets and then remaking the bed with fresh ones. He moved the nightstand back where it belonged and picked up the disheveled linens, including his discarded costume. He found her corset hanging off the dresser and looked at the torn edges. He remembered getting impatient with the tiny hooks last night, but had he really ripped her top off her?

He shoved the ruined garment in with the rest of the dirty laundry and walked out onto the back porch to start a load of wash quickly, before she saw the evidence of what he'd done last night.

When she emerged from the bathroom, the towel wrapped around her torso barely covering her damp, warm skin, he tried to avert his eyes. Somehow, the act of getting ready together seemed way more intimate than anything they had already done last night and, until she told him otherwise, he wanted to respect her privacy.

He took a cold shower, then put on a fresh pair of jeans and a clean T-shirt. When he came out to meet her, she was in the living room, folding up the quilt, a slight blush tinting her cheeks.

"Are you ready to go?" he asked.

She took a look around the room—probably to ensure they'd left no other trace of their passionate night—and said, "All set."

He opened the passenger door of Nana's Oldsmobile, and she slid inside. "Listen…" he started, but she held up her hand.

"You're not going to apologize again, are you?"

"Actually, I wasn't. I just wanted to say thank you. For last night and, well, for everything."

She tilted her head and smiled at him. "Do you think they'll notice anything is different about us?"

"Who? Our friends or the kids?" He walked to the other side of the car and got in.

"Ugh, I hope the kids don't notice." She slid on her sunglasses, and he could no longer read her expression. "I meant Maxine and Cooper."

Instead of answering, he made a big pretense of trying to drive in Reverse and avoiding the potholes as he backed down the driveway. Why didn't she want the people closest to them to know that things had now changed between them? Drew thought they had changed for the better, but maybe she didn't feel the same way.

The plan had been for her to move out at the end of summer, and he'd been fine with that before last night. But now, the thought of her departure left an ache the size of a small hole in his heart.

Just then, the other growing hole inside his body rumbled again, and she laughed. "Sorry, my stomach is pretty much running on empty."

"Drew, I think your stomach is *always* running on empty."

He smiled. He could manage small banter. But it wasn't like him to avoid an important issue. Hadn't he been the one last night who insisted on her talking about what had happened between them? He usually liked to address things right off the bat, but now he couldn't change the subject quickly enough.

"I'm a growing boy," he said. "I need my food."

"You know, speaking of food, I was doing some research on PTSD."

"Really? Why were you doing that?"

"Because I wanted to learn more about what you do." Apparently she had taken a definite interest in his job, and maybe, in turn, in him. That hole in his heart began to close up. "Anyway, I came across this article about soldiers taking culinary classes as a sort of therapy, and was curious whether your team offered anything like that at Shadowview Hospital."

"Yep, I've heard about that. There are so many helpful types of therapy out there. We already have a yoga class, a canine companion group and a creative-art group." He made a left onto Snowflake Boulevard. "But with so many patients and so many personalities, we were looking into expanding some of the treatment options we provide."

"Oh, good. Because I was talking to Freckles the other day when I was having lunch at the Cowgirl Up Café, and she said she'd be more than happy to volunteer to teach you—I mean, your patients—some basics in cooking. If, you know, you'd be interested in offering something like that."

"That would be great, actually. Captain Donahue is really into baking and recipes and stuff. I bet she'd like to spearhead a project like that."

"Um, Drew, I was thinking that maybe you could lead the group. Or at least take part in it."

"Are you saying you don't like my cooking?" What else didn't she like about him? He parked the car behind the Sugar Falls Cookie Company and unbuckled his seat belt before he looked at her.

"Of course not," she said a little too quickly and then put her hand on his arm, as if to pat him. "You're a great cook."

"Really?" he asked, knowing she was full of it, but wanting her to keep consoling him with her touch.

"No. Not really. But you're better than me." She smiled, and he couldn't help but lean toward her for another kiss. She met him across the armrest, and he decided that as long as she kept touching him like this, kissing him like this, he'd volunteer to lead any kind of therapy class she wanted.

He had practically pulled her onto his lap when an eight-year-old hand knocked on the window. "Hey, you guys better hurry. They're all out of the plain waffles, but Mrs. Maxine says they still have the ones with the nuts."

Kylie blushed and scrambled to open her door. She was probably embarrassed that the kids had seen them together. Drew adjusted his jeans, then got out and followed her up the stairs to Cooper and Maxine's apartment, a little confused by her reaction.

In fact, weren't they *supposed* to be acting all in love, like their marriage was real? In his opinion, making love last night just made their roles that much more believable.

"Drew, my mom just called," Kylie said to her husband as he helped the boys finish stacking their Jenga pieces into a tower. It had been only three weeks since they'd started sleeping together, and already she was getting used to thinking of him that way. "She said my dad is on his way to Boise State this evening to scout one of their pitchers, and he plans on stopping by my condo to check in on Kane and then swinging by here to say hi."

"Just to say hi?" Drew lifted a brow at her but continued to stack wooden blocks, his crooked right pinkie at risk of knocking down the tower.

He was so cute when he played with the boys, and even cuter after they put the twins to bed. Without either of them saying a word, he had easily transitioned into the master bedroom with her and, although they'd stuck to the same daily routine with the kids, their evenings alone had become much more entertaining.

"Well, she *says* that, but I think we all know he's dropping in to size up the situation and see if everything's going well. He's always checking in on me unannounced like this. But at least my brother is getting one this time, too. Surprise inspections, Dad calls them."

"I thought your dad was drafted into the major leagues straight out of college. Was he actually ever in the military?"

How sweet that Drew had taken the time to do research on her family. Maybe he wanted to investigate how deep the craziness ran before he got himself in too deep with her. It probably hadn't taken him much work to figure it out, though. Her family might be a little quirky, but she loved them to pieces. Especially her dad. "Nope. He just likes to remind his kids that he runs the ship."

"So," he said, standing up and walking toward her. He pulled her into his arms and kissed her neck. She commanded herself to breathe and wondered if she would ever get used to the feeling of his large hands splayed around her waist. Or his lips on her sensitive flesh. "Have any of your previous boyfriends failed a surprise inspection?"

"Are you kidding? As if I wasn't smart enough to keep my dates as far away from my father as possible. Not that

I really kept men around long enough to get to the meet-my-parents stage." She blushed, still apprehensive about the fact that Drew was the first man she'd slept with and her lack of sexual experience.

"Your mom's personality is way lower key. They have an interesting dynamic."

"Oh, trust me, my mom just allows my dad to *think* he's running the show."

Drew started pulling items out of the fridge. Thank goodness he hadn't taken offense at her therapy-cooking suggestion. Things had definitely improved in the bedroom *and* in the kitchen. Kylie dreaded the day it would all end.

"He's not one of those antifeminists, is he?"

"Actually, he's the opposite. He always told me that if his sons could do something, his daughter could do it ten times better. But he doesn't get all the fuss with women's fashion or what he calls 'female flash and glitz.' He couldn't understand why I would want to go out for the cheerleading squad when there was a perfectly good softball team at my high school. In fact, he raised a big fuss with the league about trying to get me on the boys' baseball team. When I told him I didn't want to play, he asked me why I would want to cheer for a team when I could *be* a star player. I'm the only girl, yet he's always acted as though he wants me to be one of the guys."

"Well, there is definitely nothing masculine about you."

"Pshh. I think I overdid it on my rebellion because I went completely opposite. It doesn't get much more girlie than me."

"I like all your girlie parts," he said with a wink. The Jenga tower collapsed with a deafening bang and they were reminded the boys were nearby. "So what time will he be here?"

"Less than an hour."

"Wow. That definitely is a surprise inspection."

"I think my mom felt sorry for us and decided to blow his cover at the last minute. Like I said, she's the one who really runs things. Can I help you with dinner?" She picked up a box of pasta and he practically tore it out of her hands. Was he that afraid of her cooking?

"How about you make the salad?" He pointed to the head of romaine sitting on the counter.

Hmm. Salad duty.

Lately, she'd been hoping things would keep progressing between them. She didn't know if she was ready for anything permanent, but she felt a sudden need to prove to Drew that she was capable of so much more than assisting him around the house and with the kids and the groceries.

"Well, Doc, if that psychology career doesn't work out for you, I'm sure they could find a place for you in the mess hall," Bobby Chatterson said after finishing his second helping of chicken cacciatore.

Drew was impressed with how easy it was to follow some of the recipes Freckles had been writing down for the PTSD cooking group. But thank goodness he'd gone to Duncan's Market yesterday and stocked their pantry. His new father-in-law could eat like a bear.

He'd also witnessed a softer side to the man, who, during the meal took the time to explain patiently to Aiden and Caden why it was important for them to go to college first instead of trying to get drafted into the major leagues straight out of high school. By the time he'd finished, he had the boys convinced they would have no problem becoming both Harvard scholars and professional athletes. The man had high expectations not just of his daughter but of everyone.

"So, Jellybean, does this husband of yours know his way around a dishwasher, too?"

"Dad, knock it off. I'm more than capable of cleaning up a kitchen. Maybe you should go check out Drew's workout equipment in the boat shed. Did you know he's a great boxer?"

Other than the punching bag he'd been using with less frequency lately, Drew wasn't exactly sure how Kylie knew about his boxing ability. But judging by the defensive way she'd just squared her shoulders, his wife was apparently trying to prove his masculinity to her father.

"Well, I'll believe that when I see it." Mr. Chatterson winked at him before getting up from the table. He held the back door open, and Drew followed him out of the cabin, feeling like a lamb being led to slaughter.

They hadn't gone more than a few yards when his father-in-law leaned in and whispered, "Did you see what I did there, son?"

Drew looked back to the cabin. "What you did where?"

"Oh, boy. I can see they didn't teach you much in all those fancy doctor classes. Back there? In the kitchen? That's called reverse psychology."

He wouldn't define it as a textbook example, but Drew was curious to see where the man was going with this.

"My baby girl is as smart as all get-out, but she falls for it every dang time. Try to suggest she can't do something and she bends over backward to prove you wrong. And now that she's taken you under her wing, she's gonna get her dander up and protect you."

Apparently, the ability to manipulate his daughter didn't work all the time, because Coach Chatterson hadn't convinced her to dress more conservatively or quit the cheer team. "So you're saying you were trying to get her to do the dishes on purpose?"

"Yep. I haven't had a chance to get to know my son-in-law yet, and I figured we were about due for a man-to-man talk." *Oh, great.* As much of an expert as the man might be in "psychological warfare" on the pitching mound, Drew wasn't about to be intimidated. "Anyway, I know my Jellybean better than anyone else does, and I figured you might need some advice on how to handle her."

Did her father think Drew was doing a poor job of it so far? He opened the boat shed and gestured for Bobby to go inside. With the awkward direction this conversation was taking, he wanted to make sure they were well out of his wife's earshot. "Sir, Kylie's a strong woman, and I don't think she'd appreciate anyone handling her, let alone me."

"See, I knew you were the one. Looks as if you're starting to get it."

"To get what?"

"Reverse psychology. You gotta let her think things are her idea. She has a fiery temper, that one. Gets it from her mom." Somehow, Drew sincerely doubted that. But he let the man ramble on.

"I'm not saying you should play games with her or mess with her head or any bull like that. I'm just saying that my Kylie is special, but she's strong-minded. Now, I don't believe that just because she's my baby girl and I'm crazy proud of her. I believe that because I'm an excellent judge of character, and that one back there—" he jerked his thumb toward the cabin "—has character to spare. She knows what she wants, and she is more than capable of making sure she gets it."

A lot of what he was saying was true, yet with his questionable approaches, Drew had to wonder if his father-in-law actually knew what he was talking about. "Then, why the need for reverse psychology?"

"Well, now, sometimes she can be just a touch stubborn. Gets that from her mom, as well. And I don't like to see her miss out on something good for her or wind up regretting doing X when she should've done Y. It might sound as if I'm being a little controlling, but when you two have kids, you'll see. You just want what's best for them."

The thought of having children, especially with Kylie, brought a little tingle to the back of Drew's neck. But a good kind of tingle, like how he always felt when he was a kid waking up on Christmas morning. "So how often does this trick actually work?"

Bobby sighed. "It was easier when she was younger."

"That's interesting. According to Kylie, she rebelled and went in the complete opposite direction of what you wanted."

"That's how good I am at it, son." Bobby Chatterson smiled, his straight white teeth proudly displayed beneath his long beard.

"Wait. You're trying to tell me that when she was growing up, you tried to talk her into playing baseball because you actually *wanted* her to join the cheerleading team?"

"See, all my life I wanted a daughter. Every time Lacey got pregnant, I prayed for a little girl. Don't get me wrong. I love my boys and I'm damn proud of them. But when I finally got my little princess, I was in heaven. I'd spent half my career in a locker room and men like me and you, well, we need to be exposed to that softer, feminine side of life."

Drew was trying to keep his expression as neutral as possible. As much as he was coming to like and appreciate Kylie's father, he couldn't for the life of him see the similarity. "You think we're a lot alike, do you?"

"Of course we are. That's why I trust you enough to have this conversation in the first place. I wouldn't be giving this advice to just anyone. Let me tell you, Kylie has dated some real boneheads in the past, and if I wasn't one hundred percent certain you two were completely perfect for each other, I'd reverse-psychologize her to dump your sorry butt."

Drew almost laughed at the coined term, but just then a sharp pain exploded under his rib cage.

He winced before coming down hard into a sitting position on the wood floor.

"You okay, son?" Bobby Chatterson knelt in front of him.

The pain was already fading, but Drew gingerly felt along the side of his torso. There was no specific reason why he should've felt as if his skin was being ripped open.

Unless somewhere out there, his brother, Luke, had just felt the same thing.

Chapter Ten

Drew's head began spinning, thinking of the potential danger his twin could be in right this second. He tried not to panic. After all, if he could feel Luke's pain, wouldn't he then be able to feel if something worse had happened to his brother? Wouldn't he know if his twin had...died?

He took a deep breath and exhaled slowly, then repeated it. The ache was definitely easing, and he was able to get his thoughts a little more under control.

Either way, sitting in a boat shed with baseball legend Bobby Chatterson wasn't going to solve this mystery for him. And he certainly didn't want to explain to his father-in-law the idea of twin telepathy. "It's just a muscle cramp. I think it's going away, though. I'll be fine."

"I've had more than my fair share of those." Bobby Chatterson moved Drew's hand away. "You probably should get inside and rub some Icy Hot on it. Besides, I still need to stop by and see Kane tonight. Now that I've got you and Kylie all squared away, I need to go talk some sense into that boy."

Drew was relieved to find that standing up didn't re-trigger the soreness. He locked the door to the shed, and they made their way back to the cabin.

"So, a few minutes ago, you said you thought I was perfect for your daughter. Why?" Drew not only wanted to get the man's attention off his odd injury but also was curious to hear an outsider's opinion about the potential for their relationship.

"Knew it from the moment I asked that DJ to play that song for you two at the reception and she went all swoony."

Drew stopped in his tracks. "That was *you*?"

"You bet. I knew no matter how stubborn she was being about downplaying you guys running off and getting married, she wouldn't be able to resist a classic love ballad like that. You get that girl on a dance floor and she becomes an open book."

"Let me guess. She gets that from her mom, too?"

"Hell no. She gets her lack of cooking skills from her mom. Her ability to dance and her great taste in music are courtesy of yours truly."

Drew would have laughed if the effort wouldn't have further aggravated his side.

Although the suspicious pain had gone away hours ago, Drew had been restless most of the night. Luke was on a classified assignment and Drew was anxious to get to his office, which had a secure phone line, and pull some rank to find out where his brother was and whether something had happened to him.

He hadn't told Kylie about his conversation with her father the night before or about the possibility of his brother being injured. By the time he'd gotten the twins to bed after Mr. Chatterson had left, he'd walked into the bathroom to find Kylie soaking in a tub of steamy bubbles. He'd locked the door, and neither one of them had done much talking after that.

That morning, he kissed her goodbye and drove the Jeep entirely too fast down the mountain in his rush to get to work. After almost flipping it at the turnoff onto the state highway, Drew reminded himself that he was trying to avoid arriving in an ambulance, although working at a military hospital did have its perks.

It took several calls and a lot of red tape before he finally found out that Luke was just coming out of surgery aboard one of the navy's hospital ships somewhere in the Indian Ocean.

It took another two hours to be connected with him via satellite phone.

"Luke, what happened?" Drew practically shouted into the receiver when he heard his brother's slightly raspy voice.

"Well, our op ended prematurely."

"No, I meant what happened to *you*?"

"I'm surprised you found out so soon." Drew didn't tell him the reason he knew. And if Luke felt the same connection, Drew didn't need to tell him. "It was just a little cut. Had to have a few stitches."

"Sounds like more than just a cut to me. You had to be airlifted to a ship on a humanitarian-aid mission, brother. I've been in war zones, too, you know. Stop trying to minimize what happened as if you're talking to Mom."

"You haven't told her yet? Or my boys?"

"Nope. I just found out myself. But if you don't tell me how bad it is, I'm going to speak to your commanding officer and request that he give her a call and fill her in."

"Okay, okay. Jeez, Saint Drew, it's not like you to fight

so dirty. It's really not that big of a deal. I fractured a couple of ribs and had to have surgery to get everything back in place. I guess I'm just having a hard time wrapping my head around it all."

"You mean you finally realized that you weren't invincible?"

"Something like that. I've never worried too much about death before."

"Is that why you've been hell-bent on taking so many chances with your life?"

Luke was silent for a moment. "I guess that when Samantha died, a part of me wanted to die, too."

Drew shook his head. All along, he'd known the reason for his brother's attitude, but it'd been painful to watch things escalate to this level. "I love you, Luke, and I don't regret the fact that we all walked on eggshells after your wife passed away. But it's been a few years, and it's time someone told you that you need to face your reality. People lose their loved ones and it sucks. I can't even begin to imagine the hell you went through. But you aren't doing your sons any favors by running off to play Captain Save the World every time you need to escape what happened."

"Dammit, Drew. You don't think I worry about those boys every single minute I'm away from them? Have you ever stopped to think that maybe Aiden and Caden are better off with someone more stable in their lives?"

"No. That asinine thought hasn't crossed my mind once. You're their father. They love you. They need you. They miss you like crazy. And there isn't anyone more capable of loving them and providing for them than you. So if you think they need someone more stable in their lives, then you need to man up and figure out how to be that someone."

He could hear his brother's sigh on the other end of the

line. It was hard to be so brutally honest, but they both knew Luke needed to hear it.

"I know. You're right. The past twenty-four hours have been a complete game changer for me, and I've had nothing but downtime to sit here and make some tough decisions."

Drew's stomach dropped, and the pain in his side lit up again. His twin brother had never been the best at thinking things through. He usually acted first and improvised as he went along. Which was why Drew no longer went to professional sporting events with the guy. Drew looked at the crooked pinkie finger on his right hand that served as a reminder. "What kind of decisions?"

"Like whether or not I want to stay on the team and keep putting my kids in jeopardy of becoming orphans."

"And what conclusion have you reached?" Drew knew he could browbeat his brother to death, but Luke needed to come to this realization on his own.

"That maybe I should talk to my commander about a reassignment."

"To where?" Drew rubbed his ribs. No matter how much he believed Aiden and Caden needed their father, the thought of Luke moving the boys away just now when Drew was beginning to build a relationship with them was a real blow.

"Well, all of my stuff is currently in a storage facility near the base in San Diego. But my life, my family, is in Idaho. I can't keep uprooting the boys and taking them away from the people who love them every time a new mission comes up."

"So what are you saying?" *Please don't let it be that he's going to move the boys back to California.*

"I'm thinking the navy needs recruiters, and there's a reserve unit in Boise, so I'll speak to the CO about working on a transfer there. I haven't talked to Mom and Dad about it yet, but I figure I'll need to lie low for a couple of weeks anyway to recuperate."

"Wow. It sounds as if that might actually work out pretty well." The doctors must have had him on some serious medication, because usually Luke never was good at planning.

"Okay, enough about me. Tell me how my sons are doing."

"They're great," Drew said, actually excited to be able to give his brother a good report. "Kylie got them enrolled in this wilderness-adventure camp, and they're having a blast. She has them on a routine, and the boys are absolutely crazy about her. She's even got me doing a cooking therapy class and learning how to make us fresh, home-cooked meals. Overall, it's been a fantastic summer so far."

"Who's Kylie?"

Drew's smile fell, and he took off his glasses to clean the lenses. By checking in with periodical emails, he'd been able to avoid telling anyone in his family about his wife because he didn't know how long things between them would last. But Luke was the twins' father and deserved to know who was helping care for his children. "Listen, there's something I need to talk to you about. I kind of got married."

"I knew it!" Luke's triumphant laugh made its way through the wonky satellite connection, and Drew could imagine him pumping his fist in the air.

That was his brother's response? Not doubt? Not worry for his brother's unorthodox mental state? Not even recriminations for having a wedding without him?

"What do you mean, you knew it?" They had never talked about their bond or how they sensed things in each other. But acquiring a wife wasn't like a physical ailment or a career-ending injury to the rib cage that the other twin could simply…feel.

"I just did. It was the strangest thing. There I was, flying over the middle of the… Well, that's classified. Anyway, I was about to do a low aerial jump out of a C-130 and normally, I'd be the first person to pack my chute and launch out of the plane. But something made me pause. I hesitated and radioed in to double-check our target's coordinates. I told myself I was overthinking the mission. I was smack dab in the middle of a hot combat zone, and I was acting like Saint Drew, the great analyst. But just then, a projectile grazed the wing of the plane and the sudden force threw me across the deck of the interior cabin and halfway out the open cargo hold. We were suddenly under serious fire by some low-grade surface-to-air guns our intelligence had completely missed. And there I was, hanging out of the plane like a rag doll. One of their shots grazed me, tearing through my vest just as my team was pulling me back into the cabin."

Drew squeezed his eyes tightly closed, unable to get the image of his brother practically being shot down out of his head.

"I can sense your brain working, Drew, and there's no rhyme or reason to any of it, so don't start that what-if business. You got married and I'm going to be fine."

"Wait. Explain to me how my marriage, which you didn't know about, was somehow responsible for practically getting you killed?"

"Don't you see? My hesitation was completely out of character, but it actually saved the whole unit. There were tanks and ground units carrying antiaircraft artillery that our radar hadn't picked up swarming the jump perimeter. I knew something was off, and if I hadn't taken the time to call in the coordinates, or if I'd just done my usual balls-to-the-wall routine, we'd either be dead or the United States government would be getting a ransom call from a remote cave in… Well, again, that's classified information. Anyway, I can't wait to meet the woman who married my brother and saved my entire team."

Drew took a few moments to digest the information that his brother was alive and well. And that he'd be coming home for good. "Do you know when that meeting will be taking place? When will you be coming home?"

"I don't know. I'll keep you posted."

They disconnected the call, and Drew leaned back in his desk chair.

He was relieved and more than thrilled to know he'd be seeing his brother again soon.

But his stomach dropped at the thought of telling Kylie. They'd just started getting to know each other. If she thought the kids didn't need her, she would be out the door like a cork popped out of an expensive bottle of champagne. Yet he also knew he shouldn't keep her in the dark about Luke coming back into the picture. But he needed time. After they'd made love initially, he thought he'd have the whole summer to convince her that they should stay married. But his brother's reassignment changed everything.

He needed to figure out a way to keep their marriage together before Luke came home and turned their fragile world upside down.

Kylie had sensed a tension in Drew last night after he and her father had returned from their manly talk in the boat shed. And while she'd been dying to ask Drew what they'd said, she never really got the chance once he'd locked himself in the bathroom with her.

Then, the following evening, her husband was back

to his usual sweet but practical self—up until they were alone, at which point he seemed to lose all control and Kylie threw common sense out the bedroom window.

She must've misinterpreted his earlier mood, because things only got better as the week went on. It was probably impossible for him to become any more perfect, but seemingly he had. And if his passion grew any hotter, she would need to start wearing a flame-resistant suit to bed. Or at least not expensive lingerie. He'd now ripped several pairs of her underwear and two of her favorite bras. Not that she was complaining.

Since he had the weekend off, they'd taken the boys out and about to explore Sugar Falls. They went hiking up to the waterfall and Drew carried a picnic lunch he'd packed for them before they hit Noodie's Ice Cream Shoppe after dinner on Saturday night. On Sunday, they rented mountain bikes from Russell's Sports and hauled them up to the lifts at Snow Creek Lodge so they could teach the twins how to navigate down the kid-friendly bike paths.

It was almost as if they were the perfect little family.

"Why are you smiling like that?" Aiden asked, bringing her back to the task she was supposed to be performing— which was opening up a new box of Honey Smacks. These kids had their uncle's appetite.

"Like what?"

"Like Jake Marconi's little sister smiles at Caden right before she paddles after him in her little pink canoe."

Caden shoved his brother. "She doesn't chase me as much as she chases *you*."

"She does not."

"Does so."

Kylie sighed. "Okay, boys. Eat your cereal. We have some important stuff to do today."

Cessy Walker had talked to her ex-husband, who owned

a luxury car dealership in Boise, and arranged for Kylie to get a great deal on a slightly used SUV. She wasn't quite ready to trade in her convertible yet, but after the way her relationship with Drew was progressing, she was feeling confident that a more modern-looking family vehicle was in keeping with the direction her life was heading.

Summer camp was closed for the week before its upcoming Fourth of July camping trip, and Kylie had to take the boys with her to the dealership. They were bundles of energy when they arrived. As she spoke with the dealer, she told the twins they could look at some of the new models on display. Unfortunately, when she wasn't paying attention, they sneaked into the service department and tried to do a tire rotation on another customer's car. She couldn't fault them for being such bright and inquisitive children—especially when their abundance of curiosity led to the salesman's exasperation and acceptance of her lowball offer just to get her out the door and the eight-year-olds off the property.

After lunch, she knew they needed a physical outlet since they'd been cooped up in the car and doing errands with her most of the day. She thought about taking them swimming at the rec center, then remembered Mia was doing a free cheer clinic for children at the Snowflake Dance Academy this week.

She didn't want to ask Drew's permission, because she didn't know how he would feel about his nephews engaging in a female-dominated sport. But Hunter had gone once and, although he'd complained the entire time, Kylie thought it was good for children to experience all types of activities in order to make an educated decision about which extracurriculars were the best fit.

After all, where would she be if her own dad hadn't begrudgingly allowed her to go to the cheerleading rehearsal tryouts in high school when he clearly would've preferred to see her spending her afternoons at the batting cages with her brothers?

She parked along Snowflake Boulevard, careful not to pull too close to Scooter and Jonesy, the volunteer firefighters, who were dismounting near the hitching post in front of the Cowgirl Up Café.

"Hey Mr. Scooter and Jonesy," Caden yelled out the window. "Check out my Aunt Kylie's new car."

Her heart flipped. She definitely wasn't getting tired of being called *aunt*. Just then, she saw Kane coming out of the hardware store a few doors down, his right arm still in a sling.

She waved at her brother, and he walked over to them. He'd met Drew and the twins a handful of times, but he'd been trying to keep a low profile since arriving in town, hoping not to draw too much attention to the recent scandal that sidelined his baseball career. He smiled at the boys as they pet the nearby horses. "Your face looks kinda funny, Uncle Kane."

"Oh, my gosh." Kylie pulled off her sunglasses. "You shaved off your beard!" She had never gotten used to the extreme facial hair he'd grown when he started his major-league career. She would always see him as her baby-faced brother.

"Yep. Figured it was time for a change." Kane pulled his hat lower on his head as a car drove down the street. Kylie understood her brother's need to hide his identity.

"How's the shoulder?"

"Team doctor says I'm out for the season, and possibly the next one, as well. Dad wanted me to see a specialist, but I have a feeling they're gonna tell me I've done way too much damage over the years."

"So what are you going to do?"

"Stick around Sugar Falls, I guess. Most of the towns-people leave me alone, and I can avoid the tourists when I need to. Since I have some downtime, I figure I might try my hand at building renovation. I picked up that old property out by Sprinkle Creek pretty cheap and plan to move out there to fix the old barn up."

"Hey, Uncle Kane, you wanna go camping with us this weekend?" The boys finally came over to join them. It touched Kylie that Drew's nephews had latched on to her own family, as well.

The twins talked about the big wilderness camping trip as Kylie reached for her purse and the gym bag on the pas-senger side floor. The two-day trip was an opportunity for Alex Russell and his staff to reinforce all the wilderness skills the kids had learned.

She worried for Aiden's and Caden's safety, and for the leaders' ability to keep a close eye on the mischievous boys. But she was also looking forward to a whole week-end alone with Drew.

"I might come out if you promise to bait my fishing hooks for me, seeing as how I'm one-handed right now."

"Deal!" Both boys jumped up and down, and Kylie shook her head. Now she had to add the possibility of the twins getting hooks through their eye to her ever-growing list of camping-trip worries. Sometimes she didn't know what she would do with all these maternal feelings mani-festing inside her once Drew said goodbye at the end of summer and she was no longer their aunt.

Other times, she refused to let the idea cross her mind.

The sound of hip-hop music blasted out of Mia's dance studio across the street. "All right, boys, we'd better get to class before we're late."

She hugged her brother, then took one of the boys'

hands in each of her own as they made their way across the crosswalk.

Normally, when the class started, Kylie would've allowed herself to forget about the outside world and just get lost in the music. But today, she had promised to assist Mia, which was really better than being forced to sit on the sidelines and make small talk to the stage parents who thought their kids were going to be the next big stars.

It wasn't until the last routine of the day that Kylie was finally able to get her mind back onto a more positive train of thought. She'd been wrong about Drew being tense the Sunday before last. Things were going so well between them. She just needed to bite the bullet and have a real conversation with him about where they stood.

When the twins went on their camping trip, it would be the perfect opportunity—as long as she and Drew could keep their clothes on long enough to actually talk.

When Kylie and the boys pulled up to the cabin, Drew was sitting on the porch. Wait, that wasn't Drew. She was so crazy about the guy and so anxious to see him, she was now imagining him—like a mirage. She turned off the engine, trying to figure out who the strange man was before letting the boys out. The man stood up, and Kylie realized his resemblance to her husband was uncanny.

That was weird. Drew only had one brother and he was away...

"Daddy!" both of the boys screamed before flinging open the doors of her new SUV.

It couldn't be. What was Luke Gregson doing back so soon?

This wasn't how she'd expected to meet her new in-laws. She took a deep breath and got out of the car. She could do this.

Her legs were a little shaky as she made her way across the driveway, and she doubted it was due to the intense class she'd just taught.

"This is Aunt Kylie," Caden said, and Kylie sent up a silent thanks that the boys were there to help neutralize this awkward moment. "She was a cheerleader and we got to go to dance class with her and Miss Mia and even boys are allowed to be on cheer teams if we want to."

Maybe she needed to rethink her thankfulness.

"So Drew's wife is a cheerleader." Luke smiled and held out his hand to shake hers. "I should've seen that one coming. My brother has had a thing for girls with pom-poms ever since a squad of them rescued him one time in the mall."

Well, there was a fun fact she'd have to ask her husband about later. But right now, she was dying to know how Luke knew about her in the first place. And why Drew hadn't told her that he'd been in contact with his brother or that they should be expecting him sooner.

"Was. I *was* a cheerleader." He glanced down at her bright orange Cheer 4 BSU tank top, and she wished she had packed something else in her gym bag. Something that didn't make her appear as if she was trying desperately to cling to the glory days like a fifty-year-old former high school quarterback. "It's nice to meet you, but forgive me for not being more prepared. I thought you weren't coming until the end of summer."

"Yeah, Dad, I thought you were on another top secret mission," Aiden said as he and Caden cuddled side by side with their father.

"Didn't Uncle Drew tell you?" Luke kept one arm around both his sons but was hugging the other close to his side, as though he were protecting something. And that was when Kylie noticed the outline of a large bandage under her brother-in-law's shirt. "My unit had to cut the operation short, and I've been reassigned to a new unit closer to town. Closer to my boys."

"Does that mean you're gonna live with us all the time now?" Caden's face showed nothing but excitement and wonder.

"That's exactly what I mean. We're going to be a real family. And this time, I'm going to be a better dad than ever before."

The boys whooped it up, and Kylie tried to paste her best pageant smile on her face. But she wanted to shout that no, Uncle Drew hadn't told any of them a damn thing. But she couldn't begrudge the kids their excitement or enthusiasm.

"Did you bring us any surprises?" one of the boys asked as they ran for the large canvas duffel bag propped up against the door.

She swiped at a small tear as it threatened to overflow from her eye. Her heart was tied in knots and her emotions were bouncing out of control. She was excited for the twins, who were ecstatic that their dad was home. Although she'd never met him before, she could only imagine what Luke must be feeling, getting to see his children again.

But at the same time, she couldn't help the growing premonition that Luke's arrival was going to change everything.

"Let's get settled, and I'll see if I can find something in this ol' bag that might interest you two." He rubbed the boys' curls as they walked inside.

Wait—was he staying here at the cabin with them? That earlier premonition grew to a dark cloud that threatened to rain on the brief happiness she'd so recently found with

Drew. Aiden and Caden deserved to have their family back together again.

Even if it meant she was going to lose her temporary one. Because if Luke was home for good, then Drew no longer had to take care of the twins. And if he didn't need her to help out with his nephews...

Then he wouldn't need her at all.

Chapter Eleven

Drew pulled up to the cabin after work and didn't see Kylie's new SUV. That was weird. She should've been home by now. He got out of the Jeep and heard squeals of laughter coming from inside the cabin.

Something was off. If the kids were here, where was his wife? He took the steps two at a time and then felt that weird tingle along his rib cage again.

Luke.

He knew his brother was there before he even saw the military-issue rucksack lying open on the living room floor. He made his way to the boys' bedroom and found all three of them wrestling on the floor.

"Have you been cleared for active duty?" Drew asked his impulsive brother, who should have known better than to roll around on the floor with a couple of eight-year-olds jumping on top of him. He was just a little over a week out of surgery.

"Saint Drew, I'm under fire down here, waiting for re-inforcements, and you want to stand there and give me a medical evaluation?"

"I'd prefer to give you a psych exam, but I fear I already know what the results would be. Where's Kylie?"

"She said she was going to Patrelli's to pick up some dinner for us. Should be back any minute. Now, are you gonna stand there worrying about that pretty cheerleader of yours or are you gonna rescue your twin brother from enemy attack?"

Drew smiled, relieved. She hadn't left him. At least, not yet. He took his glasses off and set them on the top bunk before making the sound of the cavalry charge and jumping into the fray.

It was only a few minutes later when he saw her standing in the doorway of the bunk room, holding a pizza box in one hand and her chest in the other. "Jeez, you guys scared the heck out of me. I heard all the screaming from outside and thought someone had the children tied up, torturing them."

She looked beautiful, but wary.

"More like the other way around," Luke said, slowly rising to his feet and rubbing his side. "When did you two kiddos get so tough?"

Drew followed suit, straightening his uniform. He should've known better than to encourage this kind of behavior. His brother had probably torn his stitches and could've done even more long-term damage.

"Here, can I help you with that?" he asked, walking toward her to take the pizza.

"Nope, I've got it."

She was doing that thing where she acted all poised and in control, but he could tell by her false smile that something was definitely off.

"Okay, boys, let's go wash up for dinner," Drew said, then caught himself as he looked at his brother.

"You guys heard your uncle," Luke said, giving no indication that Drew had overstepped any boundaries.

The twins' real father was home now. Drew was no longer their parental figure. Nor was he the one cooking the meal. It didn't escape his notice that, as glad as he was to see Luke home safely, everything was slowly shifting. This must be what the Jenga tower sensed when it was just a couple wooden blocks shy of a possible collapse.

Everyone sat down at the table with its matching place settings, and the boys were quick to put their linen napkins in their laps.

They'd been married less than a month and already Kylie'd left her mark on the cabin, as well as on him and his nephews.

There was so much to say and yet, Drew and Kylie remained absurdly quiet.

Finally, Luke started off the dinner conversation. "Did your Uncle Drew tell you about the one time I had to save him?"

Drew flinched before looking at Kylie. The last thing he needed her thinking was that he was a hotheaded young punk who hadn't spent years in graduate school and countless hours practicing yoga to get his temper under lock and key. "Please don't tell this story right now."

"We want to hear!" the boys yelled at the same time.

He shot his brother a look, but Luke kept right on talking. "So I had just married your mom and you two were still in her tummy. Drew was on a ship that was temporarily docked in Ventura and he had a forty-eight hour leave. We decided to go to a Lakers game and had those great floor seats. Remember that, Drew? Anyway, there were a couple of young dudes sitting next to us, and they'd had way too much to drink. Drew was getting pretty annoyed with them—"

"Wait," Drew interrupted. "That's not exactly how I remember it. I believe you were the one getting annoyed with them, and I was being the calm voice of reason."

"Maybe. Anyway, they started making comments about Drew's uniform and how he looked like the Good Humor Man and trying to order a couple of cones from him." When Luke got to the part about ice cream, Kylie sat up straighter in her chair. "We were ignoring them for the most part, until they started doing the kissing cam up on the Jumbotron—you know, where they put the camera on couples and everyone cheers them on while they kiss?

"Well, the drunk guy grabbed one of the team dancers—see, I told you my brother likes pom-poms—and Drew didn't take too kindly to someone putting his hands on a female like that."

"So I stepped in and got him to release the lady. End of story." Drew passed out plates.

"Wait. Then how did Dad save you?"

"Your uncle neglected to mention that the way he got the guy to let go of the cheerleader was that he punched the guy so hard Drew broke his pinkie finger."

Kylie looked at him, and Drew couldn't tell if it was in surprise or disgust.

"So you fixed his finger?" Aiden asked.

"No. Uncle Drew's finger actually never healed right after that. The part where I came in to save the day was when they actually showed the fight on the Jumbotron. Drew was worried that his superior officers would find out and throw him the brig. So I called his commander and told him it was me on the Jumbotron."

Oh, of course when Drew looked like a raging maniac

during the story, his brother was completely fine with looking like the hero riding in to save the day.

"So, boys," Drew said, "the moral of the story is, don't lose your temper and get in a fight with someone, or it might get broadcast on ESPN later, and your brother could get in big trouble with his boss."

"But you were saving the cheerleader," Caden said.

All these years, Drew had seen the moment as him losing his cool and acting without thinking. Afterward, he'd immediately given up boxing, worried he was fostering a penchant toward fighting, and had taken up yoga as an alternate way to redirect his stress. Funny, but hearing an eight-year-old sum it up as an honorable act put things into a different perspective.

As they ate their pizza, Luke and the boys were laughing and telling stories, oblivious to Kylie's discomfort, or the fact that she'd barely touched her own food. Drew glanced from his brother to his wife and then back to his brother. He hadn't expected everything to change so soon, and he felt like a jerk for not having taken the time to explain everything to her. She was probably calculating the exact moment she could leave.

The second the boys pushed their plates away, full of pizza, she immediately stood up and started clearing the dishes.

"Here." Drew jumped up so quickly, he almost knocked the whole table over. "Let me get that. You don't need to wait on us."

"Oh." For a split second, she looked hurt. Or annoyed. But before he could get a good grasp on her expression, she pasted on a perfect fake pageant smile. "Well, in that case, I better be on my way."

"On your way where?" he asked, his voice sounding

a bit too edgy. He returned her phony smile, not wanting her to think he was being too clingy. Or worse, desperate.

"Um, back to my condo. I figure you guys all probably need some time to catch up and do more male bonding."

"What about Kane?"

"His doctor told him he's going to be out at least another season, and he's decided to stay in Sugar Falls a bit longer. He closed escrow on that old property out by Freckles's house and moved in there last week."

Why hadn't Kylie told him this before? Had she secretly been planning to move home all along?

"Hey, Dad," Caden said, completely unaware that his uncle's life was unraveling right before their eyes. "There's supposed to be a UFC match on TV tonight. We should watch it so you and Drew can learn some tips to take on me and Aiden."

Luke grabbed one kid under each arm to carry them over to the couch and turn on the television.

This was Drew's opportunity to stop Kylie, to talk her out of leaving. But it wasn't as if they could have a marital heart-to-heart conversation here in the testosterone-filled living room. And after that little dinnertime story, he figured she thought all the Gregson men were a bunch of fighting heathens. He took off his glasses and wiped them on the edge of his T-shirt.

"Maybe we should step outside so we can talk about things more," he suggested, but he didn't want to push her. He'd taken her dad's warning seriously and had seen first-hand how she reacted when someone tried to force her to do something she didn't want to do.

"What's there to talk about?" She was standing very stiff and tall, as if she was already prepared to do battle. Maybe he should just let her go home and call her in the morning. He was often telling his patients that they didn't have to make any big decisions overnight.

"I don't know. About us? About how—" he glanced over the trio gathered around the television "—things might be a little different now?"

"It's not as though anything has changed. I mean, we were all expecting this at some point, right? I guess we're all just off the hook sooner than expected." Then, still wearing that fake pageant smile, she turned and walked out the door without giving the boys their normal three-hug goodbye.

He longed to beg her to stop—but Drew had a feeling Kylie had already made her decision.

"I could tell he wanted to get me outside so he could give me my walking papers in private," Kylie told her friends, who had driven straight over to her lakefront condo when she'd called them, crying. "He was probably worried that the boys were already too attached to me and didn't want them to see me leaving. One minute he was rolling on the floor with his brother, playing like a couple of overgrown golden retrievers, and the next, he kept insisting he could do the dishes and I no longer had to wait on them. It was pretty clear the whole situation had changed and he didn't want me around. He might as well have been wearing a shirt that said Pseudo-Wives No Longer Needed."

"Don't you think you're being a little dramatic?" Maxine asked, opening a bag of potato chips and handing them to her. Normally Maxine was the one who needed the chips during times of stress. Right now, Kylie only wanted a gallon of ice cream.

"No, I think I'm being pragmatic," she said as she got off her Italian-leather sofa and went to her rarely used stainless steel Sub-Zero refrigerator to look inside the freezer. Empty. Kane must've taken her stash with him when he moved out this afternoon. "I'm looking at the facts and they all add up."

"What facts?" Mia reached into a brown paper bag and pulled out two cartons of macadamia-nut brittle. "Noodie's was closed so I picked up your favorite Häagen-Dazs on my way over. Anyway, it seems to me as if you've got no concrete proof. Just mere speculation."

"Fact one," Kylie said before prying the lid off with her teeth as she grabbed a spoon out of her utensil drawer. "He asked me to move in with him to help with the kids. Not because he wanted to give our marriage a shot. Fact two. We've been physically intimate for the past few weeks, yet he's never once told me that he wanted anything more out of our relationship."

"But you've been acting so much happier ever since Chuck Marconi's birthday party. I thought the plan worked."

She licked her spoon clean, then reached for the bag of chips. Maybe she needed both. "Well, not exactly. I mean, there were some things we resolved, but we never talked about the specifics or came to any kind of understanding."

"Then, what kind of understanding did you come to?" Mia asked.

"I bet I know exactly what kind." Maxine snickered, and Kylie threw a chip at her giggling friend. "Seriously, though, you thought you could just spend the whole summer with the guy, living together as man and wife, but having no real conversation about what either of you expected out of the relationship?"

"Not the whole summer. Actually, the boys had that camping trip this weekend, and I was kind of thinking that it would be a good opportunity for us to talk things out since we would finally have some time alone."

"Sounds as though you guys were using your alone time for other purposes. Hey, stop throwing those at me. You're wasting perfectly good chips."

"We've only had quick moments when we're able to get away and, well, we don't do so much talking when we're locked in the boat shed or the bedroom or the Nanamobile."

"Eww!" Mia covered her ears. "Not the Nanamobile!"

"Fact three," Kylie said louder as if that would get her brain, and her friends, back on track. "He never even told me that Luke was coming home early. Apparently he knew about it and didn't give me the slightest bit of warning."

"So you think he was purposely deceiving you?" Mia leaned forward, her antennae suddenly up.

"I don't know if *deceiving* is the right word. But he didn't tell me, which means he didn't want me to know. My guess is he sensed how attached I was getting to him and he wanted time to break the news to me gently. He was totally nervous when he asked me to step outside so we could talk about how 'things might be a little different now.'"

"I don't think you should've left," Maxine said.

Kylie finished the last spoonful of her pint of ice cream and moved on to the next container. "Fact four. He was in a long-term relationship with a woman and broke up with her when she started getting too serious about marriage."

"Did he say he wanted to break up?"

"Not in so many words. But he's too polite, and I've got too much pride to stick around and wait to be humiliated like that."

"Remember when we had to have that intervention with Maxine when she was all gaga over Cooper but wouldn't make a move? Kylie, I think it's time you started following your own advice."

"I did my best, you guys. That night, after the party, I threw caution to the wind and took a huge leap of faith." She pointed her spoon at them. "And look where that got me—all kinds of crazy in love with my husband, the man who is probably writing his own psych textbook about the calmest way to dump an unexpected wife. So you guys can give me all the suggestions in the world, but deep down, I'm a numbers person. Things need to add up for me. And right now nothing does—except all these calories and fat grams I'm inhaling."

"He's a man, Kylie, not a number. Sometimes, two plus two ends up equaling five."

"Well, now that Luke's home, it's definitely five of us. So it looks as if I'm the odd man out." She stood up and threw away both empty cartons. She looked in the brown grocery bag on the counter, but there was only a container of peanut butter and a package of graham crackers left in it. Apparently her friends didn't realize she was dealing with a gallon-size heartbreak.

She broke the seal on the peanut butter and opened up another bag of chips, then dipped them into the creamy spread.

"Uh-oh, this is way more serious than we thought," Mia said, reaching for her precious jar.

"Listen, Kylie," Maxine said as she confiscated the chips. "We love you and we support you. But you're jumping to conclusions. It's late, and you aren't going to fix this by hiding out in your condo and feeling sorry for yourself."

"Who says I'm feeling sorry for myself?"

"Now, that sounds more like our girl." Mia smiled. Her friends were right. She wasn't the type of woman to indulge in these kinds of pity parties. At least, not for more than one night.

She said goodbye to her friends, then drew herself a bubble bath as hot as she could stand it. It really was nice to be back in her oversize whirlpool tub, but she kind of missed the smell of green-apple kid shampoo and the eighteen army action figures the boys left lined up along the rim.

It had been only a couple of hours and already she was missing them something fierce. She sank deeper into the water until the foam reached under her chin, and tried to count the teeny-tiny bubbles, wishing she could be counting their hugs instead.

She should've stuck with the numbers all along. She'd known things with Drew weren't meant to last. She could blame the night in Reno on the booze, but she now needed to shoulder some responsibility for allowing herself to become too vulnerable. Although she'd dated plenty of men in the past, she'd never let any of them get close enough to break her heart.

Her dad had once told her that she'd never be able to settle down because she loved the thrill of the chase too much. But when she'd been with Drew this past month, she hadn't missed dating the least bit. In fact, she was suddenly determined not to go on another date until she was thirty-five. Love was too hard.

If she stayed single forever, then so be it. She had a goofy but loving family, supportive friends and a job she adored. She didn't need a man, and she certainly didn't need Andrew Gregson.

The problem was, no matter how many times her sensible brain said it, the fact remained that her heart wasn't listening.

* * *

When Drew woke up the following morning, he didn't even have to reach for Kylie's side of the bed to know she wasn't there. He'd had a hard enough time falling asleep last night. He'd kept picking up his cell phone to send her a text message. But what would he say?

"Please come back"?

He remembered when Jessica had told him it was over. He'd asked her to stay, to give him a few more months, promising he would know by then whether or not he would be ready to get married. She'd told him it wasn't fair for her to have to sit and wait for him to make up his mind. If he didn't know after five years of being together, then several weeks wasn't going to sway him. She'd also said it had been unfair of him to keep her waiting, wasting so much of her time just so he could get everything squared away in his calm and calculated mind.

It was then that he'd sworn not to get involved with a woman until he knew for sure she was perfect for him. And he definitely wasn't going to suggest Kylie stay in a relationship in which she wasn't mutually satisfied.

His alarm pinged, and he looked at his phone again. No missed calls or texts. He got dressed and headed out to the kitchen, meeting his brother along the way.

"I forgot how small those bunk beds were," Luke said, rubbing his bandaged side.

"Sorry. Considering you're still recovering, I should've offered you the master bedroom last night." He made a cup of coffee using Kylie's fancy high-tech brewer and wondered when she'd be coming to pick up this and the rest of her belongings.

"Nah, I wouldn't have accepted. I missed the kids and wanted to sleep in there with them. Besides, when your new wife comes home, I'm sure she's not gonna want to share the bunk room."

"That's the thing. I don't think she's coming home. Well, at least not to my home. I think she went back to her own life."

"And she gave up all this?" Luke gestured around the cabin, where several blankets and ropes were strung up across the living room as a makeshift wrestling ring. "Is it because I'm here?"

"No. Well, not entirely." Drew told his brother about the deal they'd struck and how Kylie had moved in here only to help with the boys and to get her parents and the local gossips off her back. "So my guess is that you coming home early let her off the hook, and now she's free to go back to her world."

"Your *guess*? She's a woman, Dr. Gregson, not a hypothesis. When are you going to stop scrutinizing every tiny facet of your life and start living it?"

His mother had said the same thing before he'd come to Sugar Falls. "Lately it seemed as if I was doing just that."

"So then do it again."

"It's not that simple."

"Crap, Drew. *You're* not that simple. Stop overthinking everything. It doesn't take a doctorate in psychology to see that you're crazy for her."

"Of course I'm crazy for her."

Which was true. Unlike in his last relationship, it had taken him no time at all to know for sure that Kylie was the woman he wanted to be with. Yet his stupid perfectionist mind made him wait too long in order to strategize the best way to tell her how he felt.

"Well, brother, you're the one who's supposed to know all the right words for sticky situations like these."

That was his problem. When it came to his wife, he never seemed to know the right thing to say.

Kylie looked at her partially empty closet and decided she needed to retrieve her belongings from the cabin. The best time would be when Drew was at work and the boys were off in the wilderness. But the boys didn't leave for their camping trip until tomorrow. She didn't want them to see her moving out, or to ask her any questions she didn't know how to answer.

Maybe she should wait and get her stuff this weekend, while they were gone. She had plenty of clothes and shoes to last her until then, but she didn't have any groceries. She didn't need to meet with any clients today, so she pulled out the first thing she found in her dresser drawer and threw it on before heading out to the Cowgirl Up Café for breakfast.

"Oh, no," Mia said as she sat down next to Kylie at the café's long counter. "It's worse than I thought."

"What's worse?" she replied as Freckles set a piece of huckleberry pie à la mode in front of her.

"Honey, it's a workday, and you're wearing loose-fitting jeans and ballet flats. And is that your dad's Hawaiian-print shirt?"

"So?" Kylie spooned the ice cream into her mouth, not really interested in the other part of the dessert, which she'd ordered only because it was too early in the day to ask for a hot-fudge sundae. At least this gave the appearance of eating a morning pastry.

Mia took away the plate of ice cream and asked Freckles to bring them each a veggie omelet and wheat toast. "So you're clearly not acting...or dressing like yourself."

"Fine." She took the two loose ends of the shirt and secured them into a tight knot, baring her midriff, which was currently in danger of poufing out from too much ice cream.

"Better," her friend said after rolling up the cuffs of her jeans for her. "If people think you don't care about your appearance, they'll know something is wrong between you and Drew."

"Everyone is going to find out anyway when they see that my husband kicked me out."

Freckles put their omelets on the counter. "Darlin', if I was your hunky husband, I'd kick you out, too, for dressing all dowdy like that."

"This isn't dowdy." Kylie started to defend herself, then looked at Freckles's teased hair and low V-neck shirt. Compared to the waitress, everyone dressed a bit more muted. "And I would appreciate it if you didn't announce to the rest of the restaurant that Drew and I are…ah…on sabbatical from each other."

"Hmm. Sabbatical, huh?" Freckles tapped a long fingernail on her chin. "I ain't never heard that one. Anyway, people will figure it out soon enough if you go around town dressed like a bowling team reject and eating up all my ice cream. By the way, your daddy would have himself a conniption fit if he saw you in that getup."

"Are you kidding? Dad has been begging me to dress like this my entire life. Maybe I should've played baseball and listened to him all along. Clearly he was right, and I'm not cut out for married life."

Freckles almost dropped her orange juice carafe, she was laughing so hard. The sudden attention and unwelcome stares caused Mia to squirm in her seat, and Kylie reached across the table to tug on the waitress's leopard-print apron.

"Hey, keep it down. And what's so funny anyway?"

"You are, thinking that your dad would want you any

less feminine than you've always been. Now, I've only met the man a handful of times, but I've seen most of his games. The guy is a world-class dominator on that pitching mound. You don't get that good by not being able to size up your opponents and forcing them to swing for the fences when they should be bunting the dang ball. The few times I've seen you with your old man, it was pretty clear what he was doing."

"What are you saying?"

Mia held her fork in the air, looking sideways at Kylie. "You mean, you never realized it?"

Suddenly, scenes from her childhood began clicking into place, and she was swiftly seeing things in a different light. No wonder her dad always gave in to her demands so easily. They were his ideas in the first place. If she hadn't loved the man so stinking much, she would have been fuming.

"Darlin', seeing as how you're married to a professional head doctor, I would've thought you understood all about reverse psychology."

"Did you catch on to it, too?" Kylie asked her friend.

Mia nodded. "I had my suspicions way back in college. We were all staying at your house for Christmas break once, and you lost your temper with him when he told you he thought you should be an airline pilot or an oil-rig engineer so you could live life in the fast lane and see the world. You know I love you, but sometimes you can get all fired up when people try to tell you what you should and shouldn't do. When you came back downstairs and announced you were going to become an accountant, he waited until you walked out of the room before smiling that big grin of his and telling your mom that at least you would have a career that settles you down and keeps you grounded."

"Of all the manipulative, underhanded, conniving..."

Freckles interrupted her tirade. "Can you blame the man for wanting what he thought was best for his only daughter? He loves you. And when he requested that song for you and Dr. Gregson at Maxine and Cooper's reception, I've never seen a father more content."

"That was *him*?"

Just then, the minihorseshoe wind chimes dinged above the café door, and her husband's twin walked in with his sons.

"Aunt Kylie," the boys yelled in unison before running toward her.

"Are we going to another costume party?" Aiden asked. "Is that why you're wearing that ugly outfit?"

Okay, really, it was not that bad. She thought people would have preferred her dressing like this.

She greeted Luke, then introduced him.

"I haven't had biscuits and gravy in longer than I can remember." He smiled his most charming smile at Freckles. "So I thought I'd bring the boys out for breakfast."

"Well, if your brother thought he could send you in here to smooth talk me out of my secret recipe, he's got another think coming. Tell him he'll have to keep bringing me back to teach at those therapy sessions if he wants to learn how to make my gravy."

Luke laughed, but as much as he resembled his twin, Kylie's heart didn't do cartwheels like it did when Drew smiled. "Kids, go find us a good table and look at the menu. I want to talk to your aunt for a sec."

"Well, I'm late for dance class." Mia stood abruptly and was out the door before Kylie could yell *traitor*.

Freckles picked up a coffeepot and moved on to another table, also abandoning her. Kylie squared her shoulders, waiting for the other cleat, or in this case, combat boot, to drop. She'd already found out that her dad had been bamboozling her this whole time. What else was she about to learn?

"You took off so quickly last night, I never did get a chance to thank you for stepping up to the plate and helping out with my children this summer."

Oh, was that all this was about? She leaned back on her counter stool. "Please. No thanks are necessary. The boys are adorable, and I loved spending time with them."

"What about their uncle?"

"What about him?"

"Do you think he's adorable? Did you enjoy spending time with him, too?"

She bit her lip, wondering what his purpose was in asking her such an intimate question.

"Because I'm hoping you did. I don't know if you've noticed, but Drew can be a little straitlaced."

She took a sip of her juice. "Yeah, I kind of *did* notice that."

"He's a great listener, but he's never been the type to open up about his feelings. He doesn't usually get emotionally invested in people until he has mentally examined the relationship from all angles."

"So what does this have to do with me?"

"Because with you, he's not really himself. Which isn't necessarily a bad thing. I was hoping that maybe you could be a voice of reason for him, because I don't want to see him lose a good thing."

Was this guy talking in code to her? "A voice of reason? About what?"

"Jeez, infiltrating an enemy camp under heavy fire is easier than communicating with either of you two. Look, you're an accountant, right?"

"Yes."

"Then, let me break it down for you like this." He motioned to Freckles to bring him a pen, and then wrote an equation down on her paper napkin. "KYLIE + DREW = A GOOD THING."

She read the words, and her heart did another cartwheel. But how could her brother-in-law be so sure? "Did he tell you that?"

"He didn't have to."

"But you said he's doesn't open up about his feelings. If he's that hard to read, then how do you know?"

"Oh, he's not that hard for *me* to read. I'm his twin, remember? Anyway, I just wanted to let you know that I'm going to go on that camping trip with the boys tomorrow, and Drew is going to be home at the cabin, stewing in his own misery. Alone."

He picked up a slice of her wheat toast before standing up and giving her one last piece of advice. "But when you stop by to talk some sense into him, maybe don't wear that outfit."

Chapter Twelve

There was no point in Kylie staring at her home computer screen any longer. She hadn't been able to concentrate on any figures this morning. She was tempted to drive into town for another pint of ice cream, but she'd had enough wallowing in misery. Plus, yesterday, the staff at Noodie's asked her if they could take her picture for their Customer Wall of Fame.

She needed to fix this Drew situation, but she couldn't let her impulsiveness get her in trouble again.

Kylie waited until she was positive the wilderness-adventure crew had departed before she even let herself think of going to the cabin uninvited.

But it wasn't as though she needed an invitation. After all, half of the contents of her closet were still there—along with her heart.

She hated variables and uncertainties.

Wait. Why was she hanging back, doing all the wondering? It wasn't like her to sit by meekly and allow someone else to decide her fate. If he wasn't at the cabin when she showed up, then she would sit in her car and wait until he got home and confront him. She wanted some definite answers, even if she didn't like what he had to tell her, and she wasn't going to let her temper or her pride get in the way of finding out for certain.

She wouldn't file a tax report without having all the necessary receipts and documentation. So why wouldn't she run an emotional expense report on her marriage before making a determination of its net worth?

She was going to lay her heart out and demand he do the same. And if their feelings didn't add up, then she could go her own way knowing that she'd solved the problem to the best of her ability and hadn't made any incorrect assumptions or jumped to any wrong conclusions.

She pulled out her highest heels and her reddest dress from her walk-in closet, arming herself to conduct the most serious audit of her life. Thank goodness her father had tricked her into becoming a girlie accountant.

Drew had just dropped Luke and the boys off for their camping trip, but within five minutes of entering the too-quiet cabin, he couldn't take the solitude.

He was dying to see Kylie and was damn tired of being the patient and rational one. He needed to tell her how he felt. If she laughed in his face or gave him the brush-off, then so be it. At least he could say he'd tried. He'd already put her in enough compromising positions that one more wasn't going to hurt.

He was halfway out the front door when she pulled up in her new SUV, the one she'd bought to make all of their lives easier.

How could he not love a woman who would make those

kinds of sacrifices for children who weren't her own? His
surprise at seeing her caused him to freeze in the doorway. He should've expected her to beat him to the punch,
but maybe she was here for another reason—like to pick
up her skimpy pajama bottoms and her gardenia body lo-
tion. Well, if that was the case, she was about to get a lot
more than that. No more analyzing. He was going to tell
her every single thing he'd been thinking since he met her
that night in Reno.

"You're beautiful," he said the moment she stepped out
of her vehicle, holding herself like the Amazon queen he
admired. She really did look gorgeous, but then again, she
always did, since the first moment he'd seen her.

She looked startled. "What?"

"I said you're beautiful. I've been meaning to tell you
that for a long time, but every time I got the chance, I
ended up blowing things by rushing you into bed."

She approached him a bit unsteadily. Maybe it was the
heels. "You didn't rush me…"

"No, wait," he interrupted, not wanting to revert to his
usual role of listener. "Let me say what I've been bottling
up this whole time. I love you, Kylie, and I don't want you
to move out just because Luke is back. The boys still need
you. More important, I still need you. I think my subconscious has known it since that night we got married. When
you're around, I'm not my usual boring uptight self. I feel
passion and excitement—as if nothing else matters but us
being together. When you left the other night, I wanted to
beg you not to go."

Her steps slowed, as if he'd thrown her off stride.
"Then, why didn't you?"

He stepped off the front porch, finally moving closer
to her. "I wanted you to make that decision on your own.
I know what it feels like to be unsure about a relationship

and have someone try to pin you down and force you to make a choice. I knew that if I tried to make you do something you didn't want to do, it'd blow up in my face."

Her shoulders relaxed slightly. Hey, maybe this saying-whatever-was-on-his-mind thing was actually working. "Why didn't you tell me your brother was coming home?"

"Because I didn't realize it would be so soon. I promise I wasn't trying to hide anything from you. I just needed—wanted—more time to figure out a way to convince you to stay."

"And you didn't think about simply asking me?"

"I thought of a hundred different ways to ask you. But every time I had a chance, something else would come up. Even right this second, it's taking every fragment of self-control I can muster not to take you in my arms and show you exactly what you mean to me."

She smiled, and it nearly undid him.

"So let me make sure I've got all of this straight," she said. "You love me?"

"Yes."

"And you want to stay married to me, even though you no longer have to take care of the kids."

"Yes. However, we would still need to watch the twins for Luke when he goes out of town for training or recruiting assignments."

"So we would still live here, all together in the cabin?"

He could see her mathematical mind running the details, making sure everything added up. So far, she hadn't said no. Why hadn't he just told her all of this in the beginning? He closed the distance between them. "What are you thinking?"

"Fact one. I love you, too," she said. He closed his eyes, letting her sweet words sink in. "Fact two. The thought of no longer being married to you breaks my heart so badly,

Noodie's Ice Cream Shoppe would have to open a second location to handle my orders alone. Fact three. I'm kind of getting used to this aunt gig and wouldn't mind spending more time with your family. And taking care of the twins any chance we get."

What? No. She couldn't actually mean she wanted to live permanently with his brother and nephews. He stroked her cheek, letting his other hand graze her waist. The nearer he got to her, the more his rational thought process diminished. Which was the only explanation he could muster for why he was about to resort to unconventional tactics.

"Hmm. I was thinking living here would probably be easiest for you. I mean, you wouldn't want me moving into your private lakefront condo. It would be too peaceful, too romantic."

"Saint Drew, are you trying to use reverse psychology on me?"

"Well, your dad told me it would work."

Kylie rolled her eyes. "Don't even get me started on that man. I've got years of grief to get back at him for."

Drew laughed and gave in to his urge to pull her into his arms. "Let me know if you need any help planning your psychological warfare. Remember, we're in this together."

She wrapped her arms around his neck and he pressed his lips to hers, finally sealing their words with a kiss.

* * * * *

Don't miss Mia's story,
FROM DARE TO DUE DATE,
the next installment in
Christy Jeffries's new miniseries
SUGAR FALLS, IDAHO
On sale March 2016, wherever
Harlequin Books and ebooks are sold.

REQUEST YOUR FREE BOOKS!

2 FREE NOVELS PLUS 2 FREE GIFTS!

H HARLEQUIN®

SPECIAL EDITION

Life, Love & Family

Travis had heard the words come out of his mouth and
been as stunned as the two men he'd come to know so well
in recent weeks. Yet as soon as his brain had processed
the audio signals, he'd recognized their unshakable truth.
If trading his Air Force flight suit for one with an EAS
patch on it would win Kate back, he'd make the change
today.

"So what do you think?" he asked her. "Again, your
first no-frills, no-holds-barred gut reaction?"

"I won't lie," she admitted slowly, reluctantly. "My
head, my heart, my gut all leaped for joy."

He started for her, elation pumping through his veins.
The hand she slapped against his chest to stop him made
only a tiny dent in his fierce joy.

"Wait, Trav! This is too big a decision to make without talking it over. Let's…let's use this time together to make sure it's what you really want."

"I'm sure. Now."

"Well, I'm not." Her brown eyes showed an agony of doubt. "The military's been your whole life up to now."

"Wrong." He laid his hand over hers, felt the warmth of her palm against his sternum. "You came first, Katydid. Before the uniform, before the wings, before the head rush and stomach-twisting responsibilities of being part of a crew. I let those get in the way the past few years. That won't happen again."

The doubt was still there in her eyes, swimming in a pool of indecision. He needed to back off, Travis conceded. Give her a few days to accept what was now a done deal in his mind.

"Okay," he said with a sense of rightness he hadn't felt in longer than he could remember, "we'll head up to Venice. Let Ellis's proposal percolate for a day or two."

And then, he vowed, they would conduct a virtual burning of the divorce decree before he took his wife to bed.

Don't miss
"I DO"…TAKE TWO!
by USA TODAY *bestselling author Merline Lovelace,*
available March 2016 wherever
Harlequin® Special Edition books and ebooks are sold.

www.Harlequin.com